X-FORCE

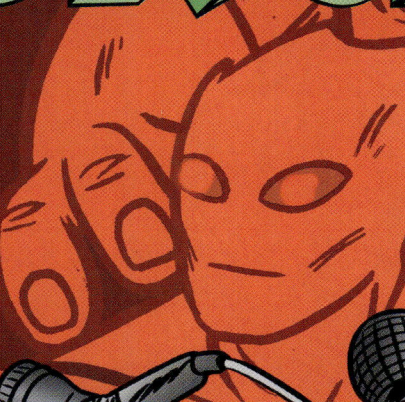

FAMOUS, MUTANT & MORTAL

X-FORCE: FAMOUS, MUTANT & MORTAL

Peter Milligan
WRITER

Mike Allred
with Darwyn Cooke & Duncan Fegredo
ARTISTS

Laura Allred
COLORIST

Doc Allred & Blambot's Nate Piekos
LETTERS

Axel Alonso
EDITOR

John Miesegaes
ASSISTANT EDITOR

Joe Quesada
EDITOR IN CHIEF

Bill Jemas
PRESIDENT

X-FORCE: FAMOUS, MUTANT & MORTAL. Contains material originally published in magazine form as X-FORCE #116-129. First printing 2003. ISBN# 0-7851-1023-2. Published by MARVEL COMICS, a division of MARVEL ENTERTAINMENT GROUP, INC. OFFICE OF PUBLICATION: 10 East 40th Street, New York, NY 10016. Copyright © 2001, 2002 and 2003 Marvel Characters, Inc. All rights reserved. $29.99 per copy in the U.S. and $48.00 in Canada (GST #R127032852); Canadian Agreement #40668537. All characters featured in this issue and the distinctive names and likenesses thereof, and all related indicia are trademarks of Marvel Characters, Inc. No similarity between any of the names, characters, persons, and/or institutions in this magazine with those of any living or dead person or institution is intended, and any such similarity which may exist is purely coincidental. Printed in the U.S.A. STAN LEE, Chairman Emeritus. For information regarding advertising in Marvel Comics or on Marvel.com, please contact Russell Brown, Executive Vice President, Consumer Products, Promotions and Media Sales at 212-576-8561 or rbrown@marvel.com

10 9 8 7 6 5 4 3 2 1

INTRODUCTION

So let's be honest, you probably don't want to read this book let alone buy it, and I don't blame you. I'll let you in on a secret. I didn't want to write it. I mean, this isn't just a comic book, it's an X-book. And we all know what that means: a rigid, established universe of mainstream characters; a Byzantine labyrinth of continuity and crossovers unintelligible to all but those strange souls who have dedicated most of their wretched lives to studying it. So when Marvel editor Axel Alonso suggested that I write *X-Force*, my immediate response was to laugh. And then, when I realized he was serious, laugh again and say, "No. Never. Impossible."

And then we started talking about how we would approach the series if we could do whatever we wanted. If I could get through all the continuity, if I could use a mainstream comic to explore real issues—in short, if I could write a story about what it would really be like to have incredible mutant powers, and then to use this as a way to explain some of the more insane and extreme elements of our media-obsessed world. And guess what? Axel and then Marvel said fine, do what you want, ditch what you want, to hell with continuity.

Before I knew it, the bastard had me agreeing to do an X-book. But a different kind of X-book; the kind of X-book a discerning, erudite and sophisticated reader—a reader not dissimilar to yourself, probably—would not be embarrassed to read, if seen on their bookshelves, or even discuss with people for whom the name "Wolverine" conjures up nothing more than a hairy mammal native to North America, and not a man-hunting mutant with side-whiskers and claws that go "snikt."

So what makes our X-book different from the others? For starters, the members of our team of super heroes are clearly more interested in fame, the fast life and lucrative merchandising deals than defeating tyrannical super-villains. The missions to save the planet are really just backdrops, the dull but necessary part of their job that allows them to continue living their fabulous, if short-lived and dangerous lives. These characters are freaks, sure. But freaks in the same way as, say, Dennis Rodman, David Beckham or international supermodel Giselle Bundchen are freaks. It's freakish to have that amount of talent or beauty. We pay these freaks huge amounts of money so we can watch and dissect their lives, and have those lives add a bit of sparkle to our own drab existences. Of course, we can't wait for them to fall over. We long for the day when they get hit by a truck or busted for their drug habit. We hate them. We fear them. And sure as hell need them.

So if you're up for a bit of post-modern deconstruction of our celebrity-mad world shot through the skewed lens of a comic masquerading as a mainstream X-book, you might just be glad that you bought and read this book. I'm almost certain I'm glad I wrote it.

Peter Milligan
Badjebupp, Australia
December 2002

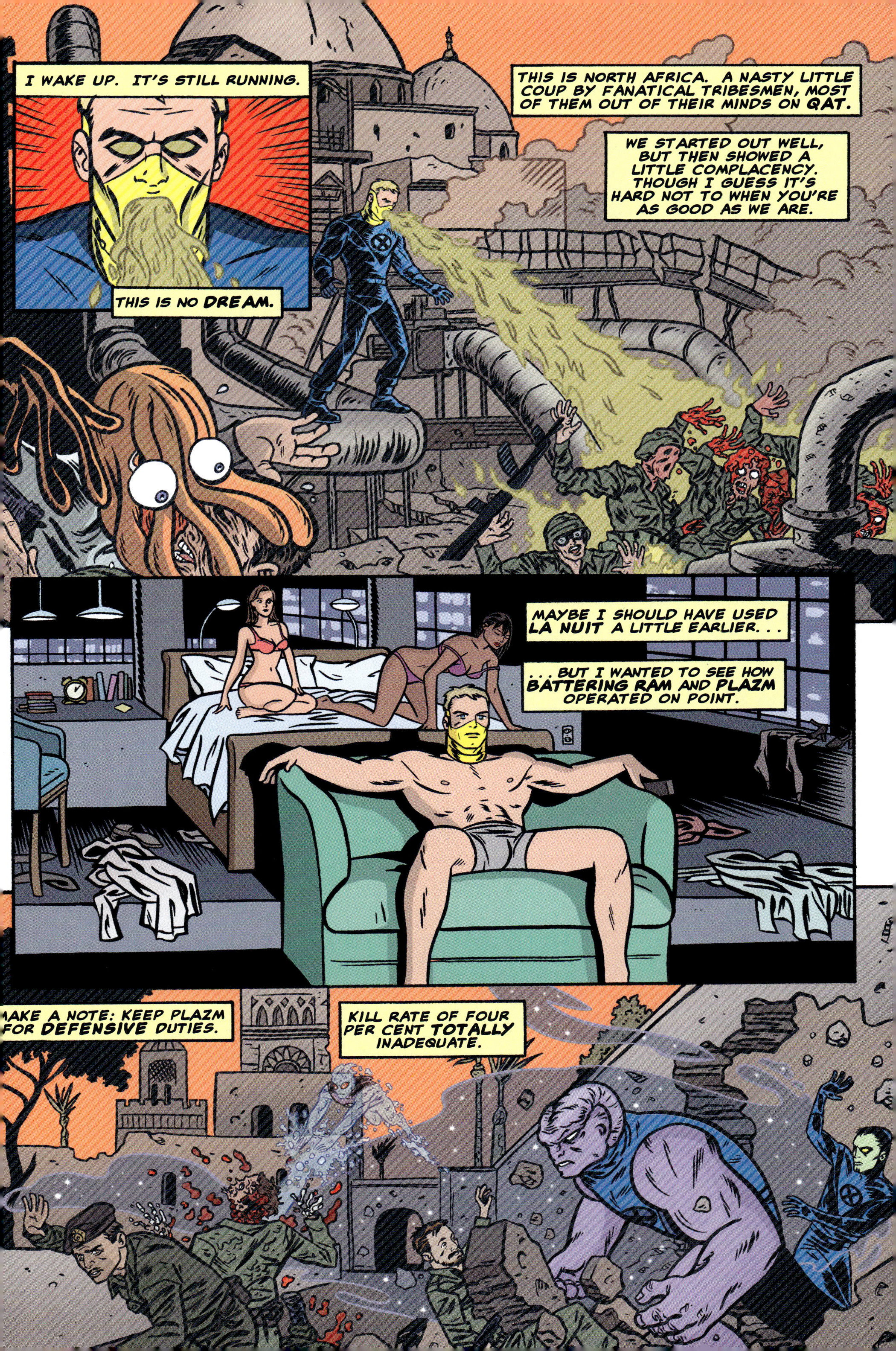
I WAKE UP. IT'S STILL RUNNING.
THIS IS NO DREAM.
THIS IS NORTH AFRICA. A NASTY LITTLE COUP BY FANATICAL TRIBESMEN, MOST OF THEM OUT OF THEIR MINDS ON QAT.
WE STARTED OUT WELL, BUT THEN SHOWED A LITTLE COMPLACENCY. THOUGH I GUESS IT'S HARD NOT TO WHEN YOU'RE AS GOOD AS WE ARE.
MAYBE I SHOULD HAVE USED LA NUIT A LITTLE EARLIER...
...BUT I WANTED TO SEE HOW BATTERING RAM AND PLAZM OPERATED ON POINT.
MAKE A NOTE: KEEP PLAZM FOR DEFENSIVE DUTIES.
KILL RATE OF FOUR PER CENT TOTALLY INADEQUATE.

eXit WOUNDS

PETER MILLIGAN-WRITER
LAURA ALLRED - COLORIST & SEPARATOR
AXEL ALONSO-EDITOR

MICHAEL ALLRED-ARTIST
MICHAEL ALLRED & BLAMBOT - LETTERER
JOE QUESADA-CHIEF
BILL JEMAS-PRES.

HE DOESN'T WANT ME ON HIS TEAM. I'M MEAN, I'M "THE ANARCHIST."
HE DIDN'T LIKE SLUK EITHER AND LOOK WHAT HAPPENED TO HIM.
ARE YOU SUGGESTING. . . ?
I'M JUST SAYING THAT. . . I'M JUST SAYIN'. . .
. . . HELL, I'M A BLACK MUTANT. IN THIS COUNTRY, THAT'S LIKE BEING BLACK WITH A LITTLE BLACK ADDED.
HAH!
WHUP WHUP WHUP WHUP
THIS IS THE POLICE. PUT YOUR HANDS IN THE AIR. YOU ARE UNDER ARREST.
UNDER ARREST?! YOU GOTTA BE KIDDIN' ME! I'M A MEMBER OF THE X-FORCE!
I CAN DO WHATEVER THE HELL I WANT!

X-FORCE CAFE

HERE WE ARE IN SUNNY **ORANGE COUNTY** AT THE OPENING OF THE TWENTY-FIRST, **X-FORCE CAFE!**

AN OCCASION MADE **POIGNANT** BY ITS DEDICATION TO THE LATE AND ALREADY MUCH-LAMENTED **SLUK.**

AS A FITTING TRIBUTE TO THAT **KIDDY-FAVORITE,** A **REPLICA** OF **SLUK** HAS BEEN ERECTED.

TWENTY DOLLARS WILL ACTIVATE THE DEAR OLD MUTANT'S **FACE THINGS**-- CAUSING THEM TO RELEASE A PLEASANTLY MILD **ELECTRONIC PULSE** . . .

SNIKT

HMM. NOW **THAT'S** WHAT I CALL **REFRESHING.**

WHAT'S EVEN **MORE** REFRESHING IS THAT **FIFTY PER CENT** OF ALL **PROFITS** WILL BE DONATED TO **SLUK'S** FAVORITE **CHARITIES!**

WE'RE STILL WAITING FOR MEMBERS OF THE **X-FORCE** THEMSELVES TO SHOW UP. THEY'VE OBVIOUSLY BEEN **DETAINED** BY SOME **SECRET MATTER** OF **INTERNATIONAL IMPORTANCE!**

OOP EANIES $5.⁰⁰

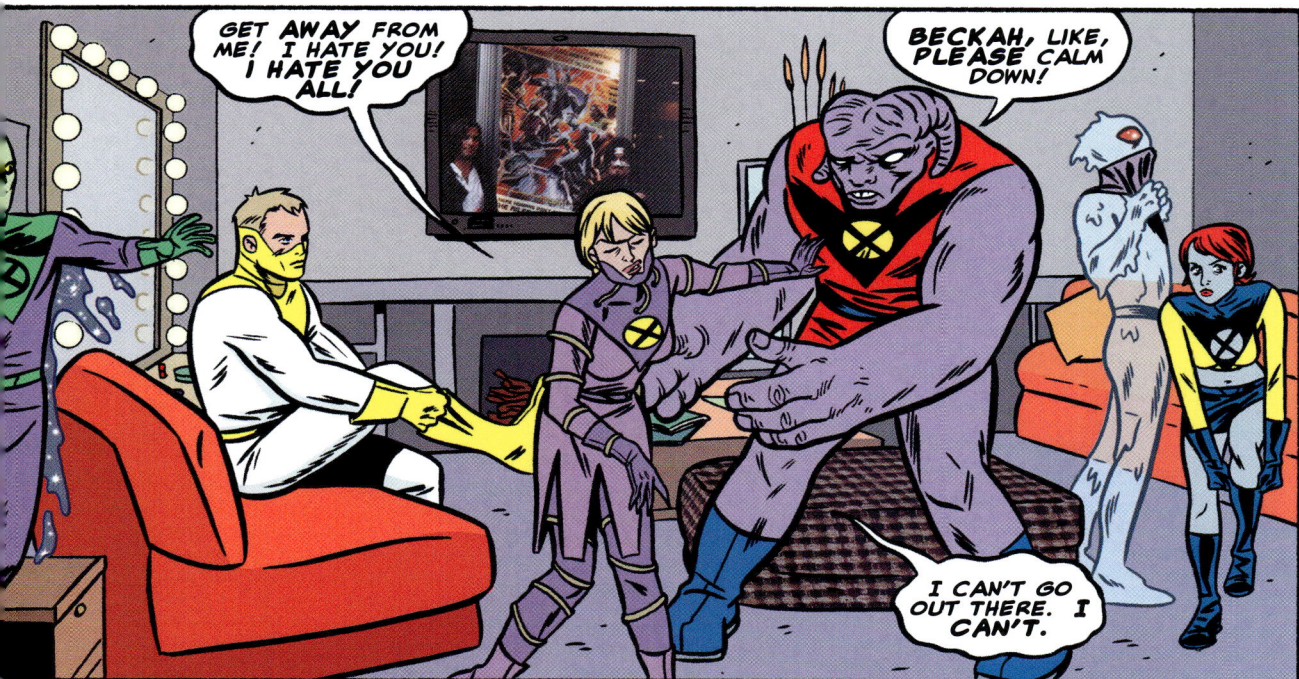

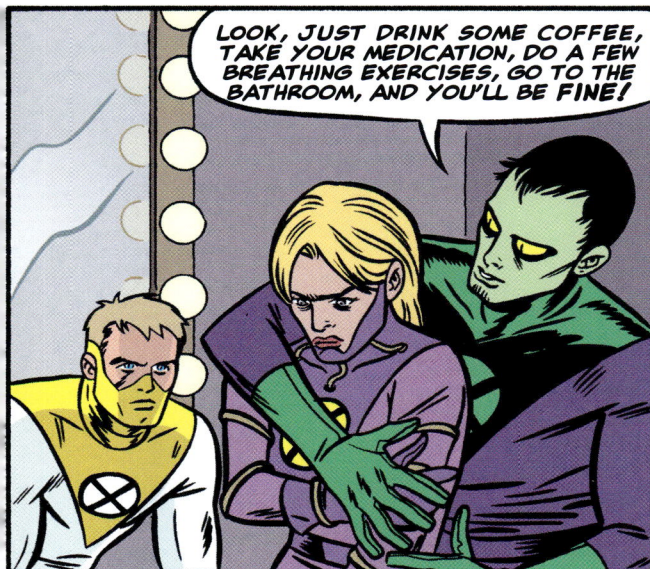

I THOUGHT THAT KIND OF STUFF WAS **EXPECTED** OF ME!

SANTA MONICA.

INTERNAL CONFLICT. STRUGGLES FOR ASCENDANCY. PERSONAL ENMITIES. ISN'T THAT THE KIND OF THING THAT KEEPS PEOPLE **INTERESTED** IN US? I MEAN, WE CAN'T BE FIGHTING BAD GUYS **ALL** THE TIME.

YOU'VE BEEN WITH US FOR **FIVE** MINUTES, ALICAR. DON'T TRY TO TELL US HOW WE SHOULD **BEHAVE**.

I'M GETTING A PARANOID VIBE. WHAT'S UP WITH YOU PEOPLE? YOU'VE ALL GOT SUCH... **CHIPS** ON YOUR SHOULDERS.

OKAY, CHILDREN, NURSERY HOUR IS OVER. WE'VE GOT A **JOB** TO DO.

HOORAY.

DON'T GET **TOO** EXCITED, EDIE. THIS IS A LONG WAY FROM BEING A **MISSION IMPOSSIBLE**.

SEE, OUR **FOCUS GROUPS** SUGGEST THAT SOME OF YOUR ADORING PUBLIC ARE GETTING A LITTLE RESENTFUL OF THE KINDS OF LIFESTYLES YOU GUYS LEAD.

THEY'RE FINDING IT A BIT HARD TO **EMPATHIZE** WITH YOU.

WHO'S GOT THE T.V. RIGHTS?
WE'VE THROWN THIS ONE WIDE OPEN. A "FREEBEE." LIKE I SAID, THIS IS ABOUT IMPROVING OUR PUBLIC IMAGE. A KIND OF. . . EXHIBITION MATCH.
DOOP, OF COURSE, WILL BE RECORDING THE ENTIRE THING FOR OUR OWN VIEWING.
DOOP, HONEY, CAN YOU TRY NOT TO KEEP SHOOTING MY BUTT FROM A LOW ANGLE? YOU'RE MAKING ME LOOK AS BIG AS JENNIFER LOPEZ!
EXIT
IT'S A WALK IN THE PARK, GUYS. SLAUGHTER WITH A SMILE. YOU MIGHT EVEN GET TO CATCH A BROADWAY SHOW AFTER.
EDIE. I TAKE IT YOU HAVE THE ENERGY TO GET US TO NEW YORK?
AND BACK!
NUMBER ONE, CAN I HAVE A WORD. . .?
LATER, BATTERING RAM.
EDIE . . .

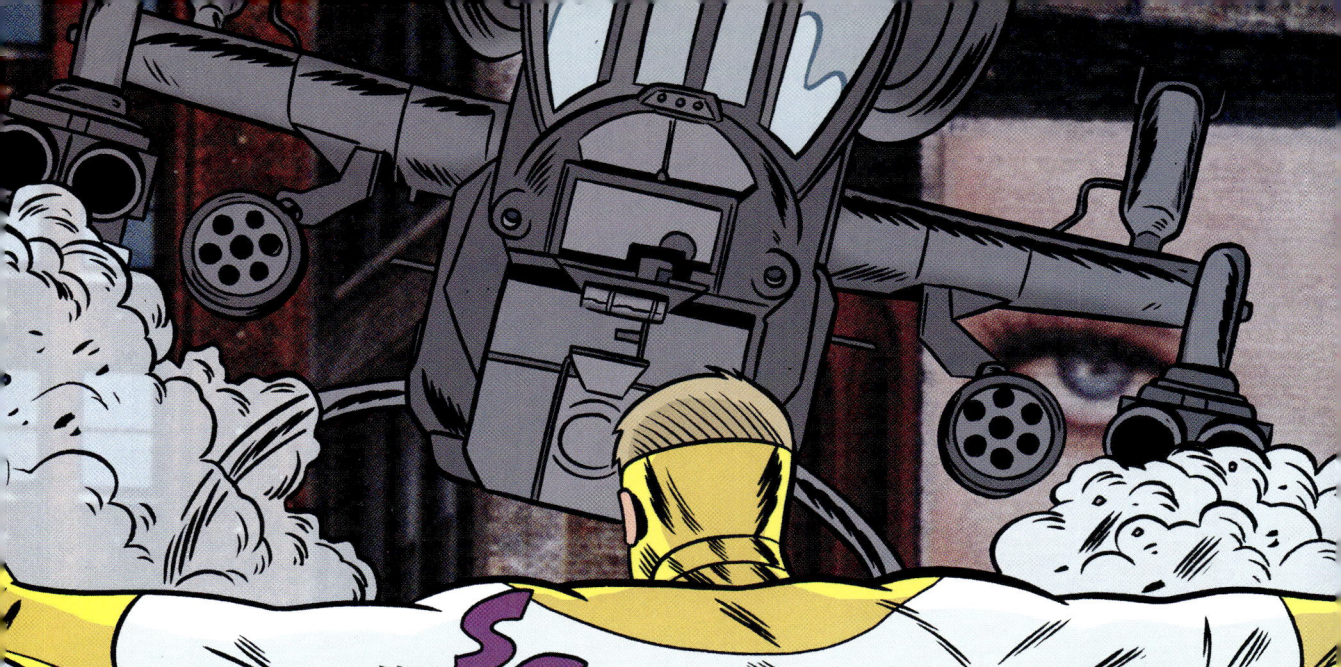

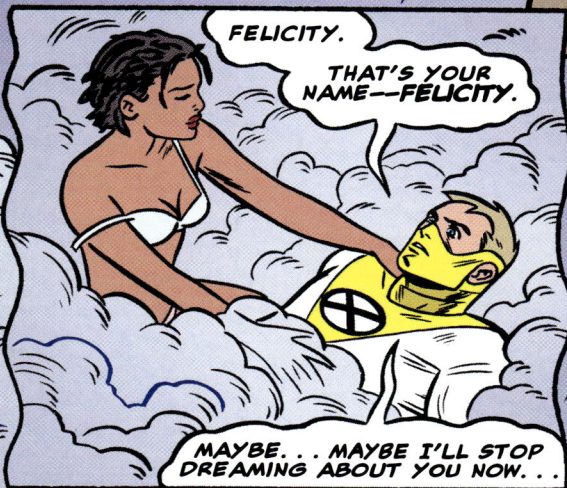

THE SHOWER IS SPECIALLY DESIGNED TO EMIT A FINE MIST, BUT IT STILL FEELS LIKE A THOUSAND **NEEDLES** STABBING AT MY FLESH.

IF I WASN'T SO SENSITIVE TO **SMELL**, I'D SKIP SHOWERS ALTOGETHER.

TO THINK I USED TO LIVE WITHOUT **THE SUIT**.

MY MIND HAS GROWN LAZY. THE DISCIPLINES I USED TO PROTECT MYSELF WITH, RUSTY.

EXAMPLE:

A BLUEBOTTLE FLY'S SLUGGISH TRAJECTORY ACROSS THE ROOM CREATES AN UNPLEASANT **VIBRATION** DOWN MY SPINE.

BUT NOW I'M SLIPPING IT ON, MY ARMOR AND SHIELD, MUMBLING MY DAILY PRAYER OF THANKS TO **PROFESSOR X**.

PEPARING FOR MY **OTHER** DAILY RITUAL.

MY FRIEND, WHO'LL BE WAITING FOR ME AT THE END OF THE DAY.

WHRRRRR

EVER FAITHFUL. THE ONLY THING THAT MAKES SENSE OF THE HOURS AND THE PAIN.

Peter Milligan-Writer   Michael "Zane" Allred-Artist

MISTER SENSITIVE

Laura Allred-Colorist   Michael Allred & Blambot-Letters   John Miesegaes-Assistant Editor

Axel Alonso-Editor   Joe Quesada-Chief   Bill Jemas-President

"SEE!

"IT WAS MEANT FOR ME!

"ZEITGEIST JUST GOT IN THE WAY, MAN!"

AXEL ALWAYS WAS A LITTLE SLOW ON HIS FEET.

I WAS MEANT TO GET IT, RIGHT?

NO ONE WAS MEANT TO GET IT, TIKE!

COACH, I CAN STILL SEE AXEL'S INTESTINES CURLING UP IN MY LAP! DO YOU WANT ME TO TELL YOU HOW WARM THEY WERE? DO YOU WANT ME TO DESCRIBE HOW THEY SMELLED?

SO GIVE US SOME ANSWERS!

NOT PARTICULARLY, EDIE.

SOME OF YOU DIDN'T COME BACK FROM THE GAME. THAT'S THE ONLY ANSWER YOU NEED.

YOU'RE U-GO GIRL AND THE ANARCHIST.

DEAL WITH IT.

COACH IS RIGHT. IF I'M GOING TO BE THE NEW LEADER, I HAVE TO BE THE ONE WHO MOVES THIS TEAM ON.

IF YOU'RE GOING TO BE THE NEW TEAM LEADER.

I MEAN, LET'S FACE IT. YOU AIN'T NOTHIN' BUT A GLORIFIED TRANSPORT SYSTEM. A MUTANT GREYHOUND BUS!

DON'T PUSH IT, MISTER.

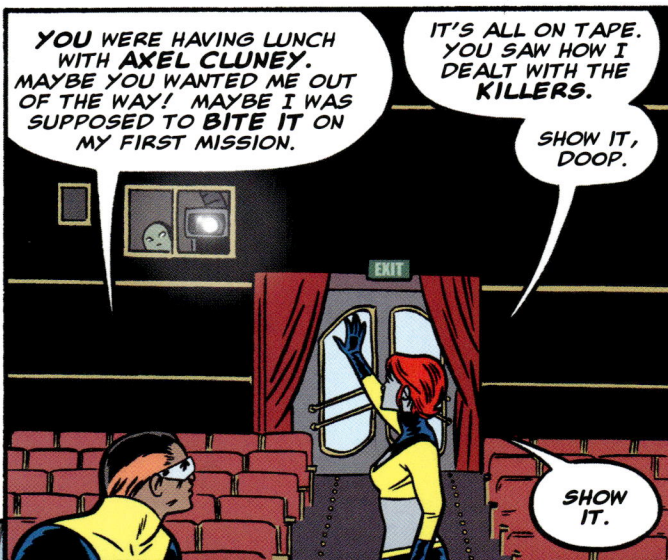

I'LL PUSH IT ALL I LIKE, SISTER.

COME ON, X-FORCE! BREAK IT UP.

YOU WERE HAVING LUNCH WITH AXEL CLUNEY. MAYBE YOU WANTED ME OUT OF THE WAY! MAYBE I WAS SUPPOSED TO BITE IT ON MY FIRST MISSION.

IT'S ALL ON TAPE. YOU SAW HOW I DEALT WITH THE KILLERS.

SHOW IT, DOOP.

EXIT

SHOW IT.

"AXEL KIND OF GROANED WHEN I LET GO OF HIM. BUT I HAD TO. I KNEW I HAD A RESPONSIBILITY.

"I WAS THE SENIOR X-FORCE MEMBER NOW.

"ANY PAYBACK CAME DOWN TO ME.

"GLORIFIED TRANSPORT SYSTEM?

"TELL THAT TO THE FLESH AND BONE THEY SCRAPED OFF THE SIDEWALK!"

SO YOU GOT THE DROP ON A FEW OF THE BAD GUYS. BIG DEAL.

BY SEPARATING THEM FROM THEIR SPINAL CORDS?

I WAS THE ONE TRYING TO FIND OUT WHO THEY WORKED FOR.

SO I GOT A LITTLE CARRIED AWAY.

OR MAYBE YOU DELIBERATELY GOT RID OF THEM, SO THEY COULDN'T TALK.

NOW THAT'S ONE HELL OF AN ACCUSATION.

I JUST JOINED X-FORCE. WHY WOULD I WANT TO ICE EVERYONE?

HOW ABOUT SO YOU COULD HIRE YOUR OWN GUYS? BE LEADER OF A NEW X-FORCE SHAPED IN YOUR OWN IMAGE?

HMM, WHEN YOU TALK ABOUT IT LIKE THAT, IT DON'T SOUND HALF BAD.

SEE? HE DOESN'T TAKE ANYTHING SERIOUSLY. NOT EVEN THIS.

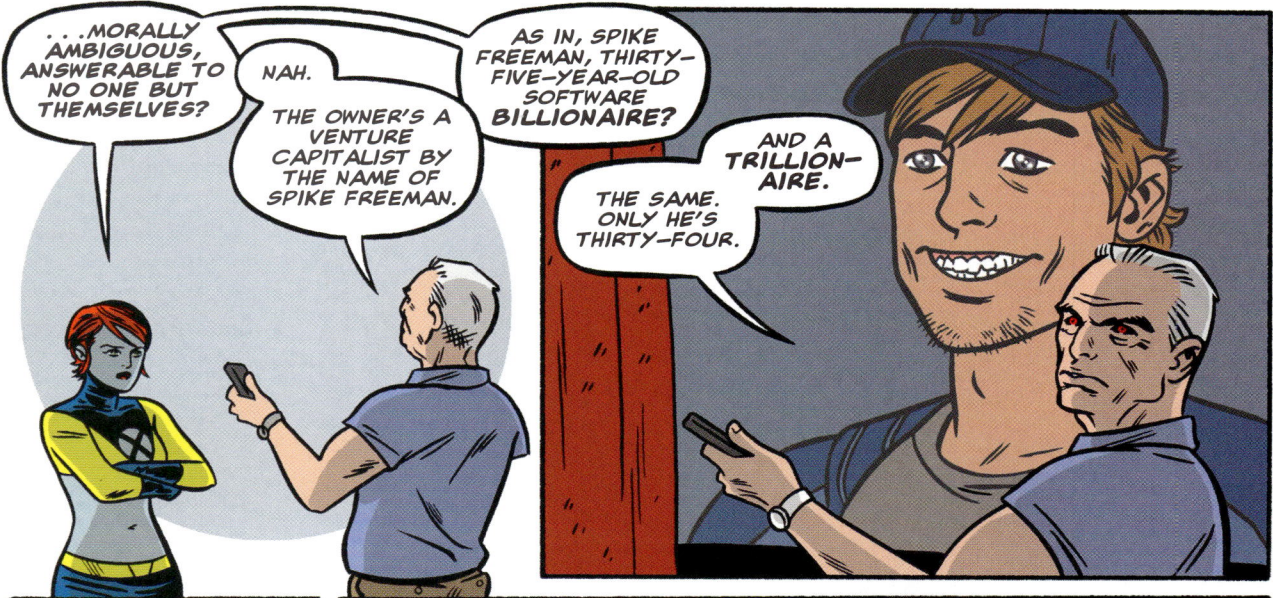

HE'S **BIG**...

HE'S **PINK**...

AND HE HAS **IMPECCABLE** TASTE IN **SOFT FURNISHINGS!**

MICKEY TORK CUT HIS TEETH WORKING AS A VIGILANTE IN THE STREETS OF SAN FRANCISCO, OPERATING UNDER HIS FORMER NAME **"RAINBOW."**

DUE TO AN EVOLVING GENETIC CONDITION, THAT NAME SOON CEASED TO BE APPROPRIATE.

THE BIG BOY WITH THE PENCHANT FOR MUSICAL THEATER AND PUMPING IRON SOON FOUND HE POSSESSED THE UNCANNY CHAMELEON ABILITY TO MERGE INTO HIS SURROUNDINGS...

...THEN **PINK UP** AND WREAK HAVOC!

NEVER BETTER DEPLOYED THAN LAST YEAR, AGAINST A BALKAN TERRORIST GROUP.

WITH A TWO-YEAR KILL RATING OF SIX PER MISSION, THE MUTANT NOW KNOWN AS **"BLOKE"** IS BETTERED ONLY BY MISTER SENSITIVE AND, OF COURSE, THE ANARCHIST, WHO HAS ALREADY MADE THE BIG STEP UP TO X-FORCE.

HARVARD.

A YOUNG AND BRILLIANT STUDENT NAMED **MYLES ALFRED** ATTENDS A LECTURE ON SHAKESPEARE, FREUD AND THE OEDIPUS FALLACY BY HIS ENGLISH TUTOR, HAROLD BLOOM.

HIS FATHER IS AN ESTEEMED ACADEMIC, HIS MOTHER A RENOWNED ETHNOMUSICOLOGIST AND EXPONENT OF THE NORTH AFRICAN 'UD.

THE FUTURE IS MAPPED OUT FOR MYLES: STUDY. BOOKS. A LIFE OF THE MIND.

BUT DESTINY, AND **GENETICS**, HAVE **OTHER** IDEAS.

AT FIRST, IT WAS TRIGGERED BY FEAR OR ANGER.

BUT SOON MYLES BECAME ABLE TO CONTROL HIS TRANSFORMATIONS AT **WILL**.

AUTHOR OF A CRITICALLY-ACCLAIMED PAMPHLET ON WALT WHITMAN AND ABLE TO TEAR THROUGH STEEL WALLS WITH HIS TEETH AND CLAWS, MYLES ALFRED IS. . .

"VIVISECTOR"!

IT WAS THE KIND OF BACKGROUND EVERY ACTOR, ROCK STAR OR MUTANT DREAMS OF.

ALCOHOLIC MOTHER, ABUSIVE FATHER, ALL WRAPPED UP IN A HEADY BREW OF ILLITERACY AND RACIAL INTOLERANCE.

TO ESCAPE THE TRAILER PARKS OF HIS YOUTH, YOUNG *BILLY BOB REILLY* TOOK TO THE *STREETS*.

THE STREETS WERE HIS HOME.

THE STREETS *ARE* HIS HOME.

TO SURVIVE, BILLY BOB DID THINGS HE WASN'T PROUD OF, CHALKING UP HIS ALARMING WEIGHT FLUCTUATIONS TO THE STRESS AND STRAIN OF *THE LIFE*.

UNTIL TESTS PROVED WHAT BILLY BOB HAD ALWAYS SUSPECTED.

HE WAS NOT LIKE OTHER MEN.

HE CARRIED WITH HIM THE MARK OF THE *MUTANT*.

AFTER RIGOROUS TRAINING, BILLY BOB DEVELOPED AN AMAZING CONTROL OVER HIS SKIN AND SUBCUTANEOUS GUNK.

AND THOUGH HE HAS PROVED AN INVALUABLE TEAM MEMBER WHEREVER HE'S FOUGHT, WORD IS THERE'S *MUCH MORE* TO BE SEEN FROM...

"PHAT."

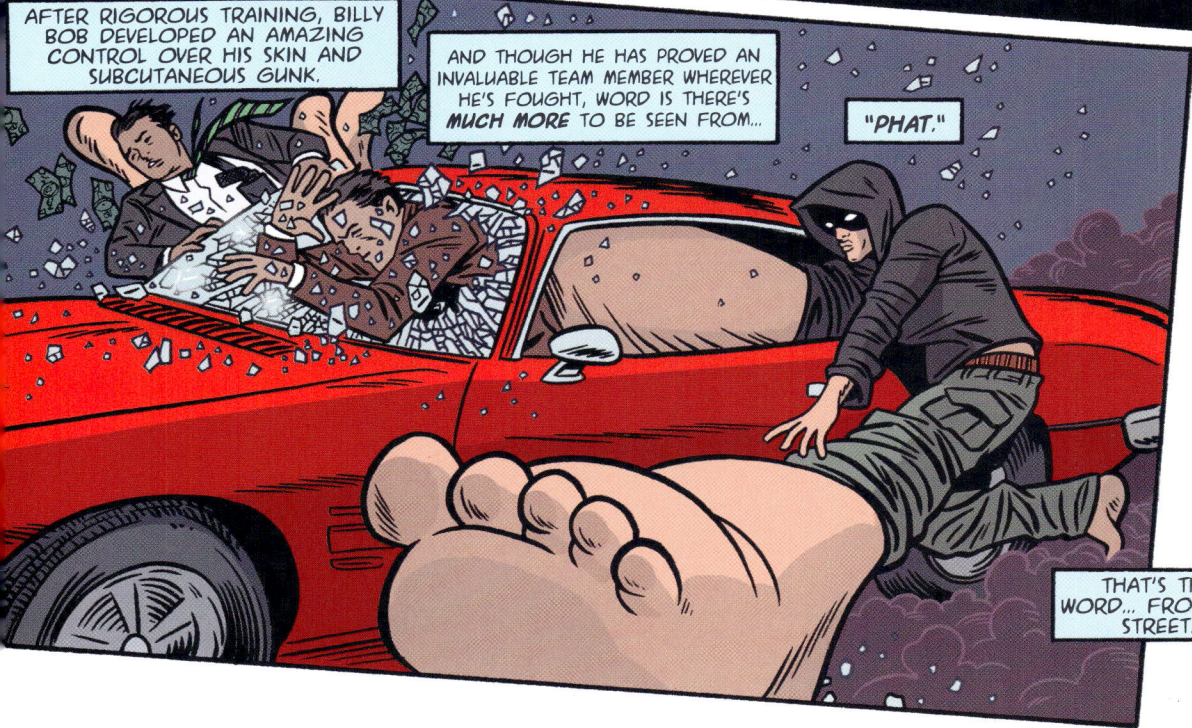

THAT'S THE WORD... FROM THE STREET.

A BARRIO IN BUENOS AIRES, WHERE THE AIR IS ANYTHING BUT BEAUTIFUL. IT'S SEVENTEEN YEARS AGO AND THE STREETS PULSE TO THE SOUND OF THE RUMBA AND WISTFUL SONGS OF THE LOST *MALVINAS*.

A YOUNG IRISH GIRL AND AN ARGENTINIAN PRIEST WORK SIDE-BY-SIDE IN A *MISSION* FOR THE *POOR*.

THE NIGHTS BECOME HOTTER, ITS RHYTHMS MORE SINUOUS.

NINE MONTHS LATER. COUNTY KERRY, IRELAND. A COMMUNITY SCANDALIZED. A FAMILY TORN.

A *CHILD* BORN.

ANNA. WITH THE GRASS-GREEN EYES.

ANNA. WHO CAN MOVE THINGS JUST BY LOOKING AT THEM. WHO CAN HEAL THE SICK AND THE SAD.

WHOSE REPUTATION GROWS.

"SAINT ANNA," THEY START TO CALL HER.

HOLLYWOOD

THEY HAVEN'T STOPPED.

YES, HE ALWAYS HAD THOSE **ANTENNAE** AND THAT SHOCK OF **WHITE HAIR**.

BUT APART FROM THAT, **GUY SMITH** WAS A NORMAL KID.

A NORMAL KID WHOSE FOLKS TRAGICALLY DIED IN A HOUSE FIRE WHEN GUY WAS JUST TWO YEARS OLD.

AND THEN, SOMETIME DURING HIS TEENS, GUY BEGAN TO CHANGE. HE STARTED TO BECOME... **SENSITIVE. VERY** SENSITIVE.

A WARM BREEZE. THE RUSTLE OF HIDDEN LIFE UNDERFOOT. THE RACING OF A GIRLFRIEND'S HEART.

PAIN. CONFUSION. ANGUISH.

THE DRUGS HE TOOK TO CONTROL THE ACUTENESS OF HIS SENSES WEREN'T AN ANSWER.

GUY TRAVELED FAR AND WIDE, STUDYING MARTIAL ARTS AND MENTAL DISCIPLINES-- TUKANG MOOSUL. JEET KUNE DO. TD MEDITATION. TANTRIC MAGIC. THE OBSCENE KISS, AND ON AND ON...

AND THEN HE CAME TO THE ATTENTION OF ONE **PROFESSOR CHARLES XAVIER,** WHO DESIGNED FOR GUY A SPECIAL **SUIT.**

A SUIT THAT EMPOWERED HIM TO TEMPER AND CONTROL HIS UNDILUTED SENSES.

GUY SMITH HAS CONQUERED OVERWHELMING ODDS TO BECOME...

"MISTER SENSITIVE."

YOU DISSIN' ME?

YO! YOU DISSIN' ME, SON?

YOU BEST COME CORREC' OR I'LL WHUP YOUR **WHITE** BUTT **BLACK** AN' **BLUE**!

OH, SPARE ME THE PATHETIC MACHO POSTURING! DO YOU THINK I WANT TO BE A PART OF THIS **LUDICROUS** OUTFIT? I DON'T WANT TO BE A **TEAM PLAYER**! AND I MOST **CERTAINLY** DO NOT WANT TO BE A **MUTANT**.

SO YOU'RE ASHAMED OF WHAT YOU **ARE**!?

LISTEN, FRIEND, YOU'VE EITHER GOT TO BE A PART OF THE PROBLEM OR A PART OF THE—

IF YOU EVER MISQUOTE SOMETHING TO ME AGAIN-- WHETHER BY **MALCOLM X** OR **PROFESSOR X**--I SHALL SERIOUSLY CONSIDER STAMP-ING ON YOUR **CORPUS CALLOSOM**.

BACK OFF, BOOKWORM!

BLOOM

THEY'RE EATING IT UP. THEY'RE X-FORCE. THEY'VE **MADE** IT. THEY CAN **SMELL** THE PROMISED LAND! I CAN SMELL IT ON THEM.

LISTEN TO THE SALIVA RUSHING AROUND THEIR MOUTHS.

DO ANY OF US HAVE ANY IDEA WHAT WE'VE GOTTEN OURSELVES INTO?

EVERYONE. COOL IT. NOW. I WILL NOT TOLERATE THIS KIND OF BEHAVIOR IN MY TEAM.

HEY, KIDS. I'VE GOT A BALL. WANNA BE ON MY TEAM?

YOUR TEAM?

NEWS FLASH: WE'RE ALL ON THE SAME TEAM. AND GUESS WHAT? I'M GOING TO FILL YOU IN ON OUR NEXT MISSION!

IS THIS GOING TO BE ONE OF THOSE "WALKS IN THE PARK," LIKE THE THING WITH BOYS R US?

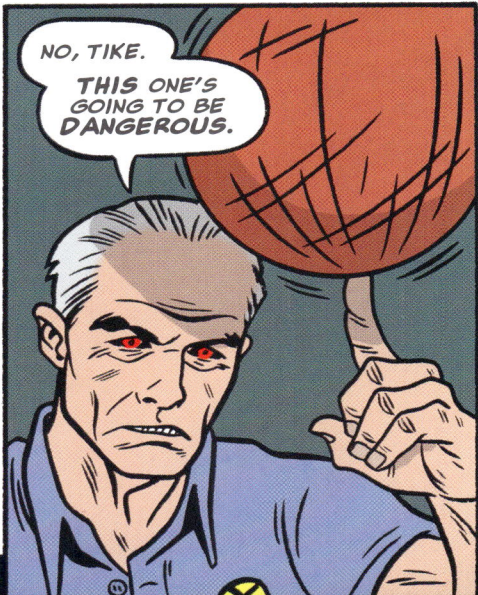

NO, TIKE. THIS ONE'S GOING TO BE DANGEROUS.

EXIT

LIGHTS, DOOP.

SAN DIEGO.
YOU MIGHT RECOGNIZE THIS FOOTAGE.

THAT KID FROM THE PEOPLE'S REPUBLIC OF BASTRONA WHOSE PARENTS WERE KILLED BY A TRUCK AS THEY TRIED TO MAKE IT ACROSS THE BORDER.

THERE HE IS. POOR LITTLE *PACO PEREZ.*

THE FEDS RESCUED HIM FOR THE REDS.

SO WHAT'S THAT GOT TO DO WITH *US?*

HAVE YOU EVER WONDERED WHY THEY WERE SO *DESPERATE* TO GET LITTLE PACO BACK?

POLITICS?

TO STICK IT TO THE >AHEM< "IMPERIALIST RUNNING DOGS OF THE UNITED STATES"?

THIS IS A CRATER IN SOUTHERN BASTRONA. IT'S HALF A MILE WIDE AND ALMOST AS DEEP.

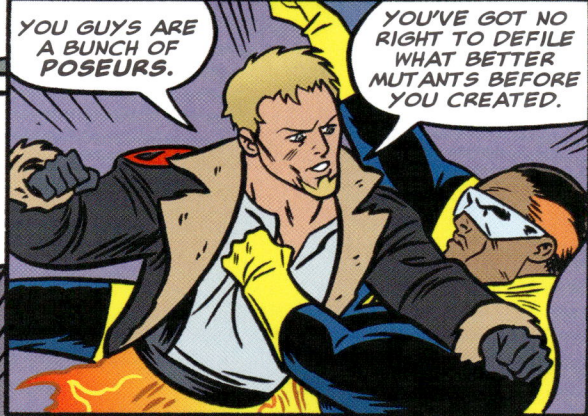

SHE'S BLUFFING. I CAN **SENSE** IT.

IT'S IN HER SWEAT. HER HEARTBEAT. A MODULATION OF THE LAST TWO WORDS.

THAT GIVES ME THE SPLIT-SECOND I NEED.

ᏋᎷ ᎧᎾ ᏬᏒᎯᏬᏬ ᎶᏧᎶ ᏓᏎᏛ ᎶᏯ ᏬᎡᏕᎤ

PICK ON SOMEONE YOUR OWN SIZE!

HEY, COACH--AREN'T YOU WORRIED THAT THEY'RE GOING TO KILL EACH OTHER?

>SIGH< DESPITE APPEARANCES, THEY'RE ALL **PROFESSIONALS.** SERIOUS INJURY IS A POSSIBILITY BUT I DOUBT THAT IT'LL COME DOWN TO **BODY BAGS.**

DO YOU WANT ME TO MOVE **INSIDE** YOU.. .TO HELP YOU WITH THE **PAIN?**

SAINT ANNA, YOU CAN MOVE ME **ANY WAY** YOU LIKE.

RESPECT! FOR A BOOK-WORM, YOU KICK BUTT!

IF I WANT AFFIRMATION FROM **YOU,** I'LL ASK FOR IT!

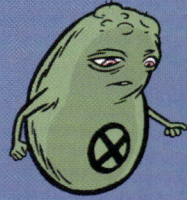

RELATIVE CALM HAS RETURNED TO THE X-FORCE PRESS CONFERENCE—AND BY THE WAY, EDITED HIGHLIGHTS OF THE MUTANT SLUGFEST CAN BE SEEN LATER TONIGHT ON PAY-PER-VIEW.

NOW IT'S TIME FOR THE COACH'S BIG ANNOUNCEMENT.

AS TO THE MATTER OF OUR NEW TEAM LEADER...

IT'S AN IMPOSSIBLE TASK TO REPLACE MY OLD COLLEAGUE AND, I'M PROUD TO SAY, FRIEND, AXEL CLUNEY— A.K.A. "ZEITGEIST"...

BUT AFTER CAREFUL CONSIDERATION, I'VE DECIDED ON THE PERSON MOST WORTHY TO FOLLOW IN HIS FOOTSTEPS.

POX 5

REPORT

THE NEW TEAM LEADER OF X-FORCE IS...

...THE ORPHAN.

THE "ORPHAN," THE MUTANT FORMALLY KNOWN AS "MISTER SENSITIVE," AND NEW TEAM LEADER OF THE X-FORCE, HAS JUST ARRIVED AT HIS HOME.
ORPHAN—GUY!—HOW DO YOU FEEL ABOUT BEING MADE TEAM LEADER BEFORE YOU'VE EVEN BEEN ON A MISSION?

SURPRISED. PROUD. A LITTLE SCARED.

AND WHEN WILL YOU BE MOVING INTO THE X-FORCE BUILDING?

SOON.

STRUGGLING IN THE AFTERMATH OF THE *BOYZ R US MASSACRE*, WITH MOST OF ITS OLD MEMBERS GONE, A POTENTIAL LEGAL WRANGLE OVER USE OF THE VERY NAME "*X-FORCE*"...
AND REPORTS THAT EDIE SAWYER— A.K.A. "*U-GO-GIRL*"—MIGHT BE FORMING YET ANOTHER SPLINTER-GROUP, RUMORS ARE RIFE THAT X-FORCE IS FALLING—

BLAM

A GUNSHOT! THAT WAS A GUNSHOT!

I REPEAT: THERE'S BEEN THE SOUND OF A GUNSHOT FROM INSIDE THE ORPHAN'S HOME!

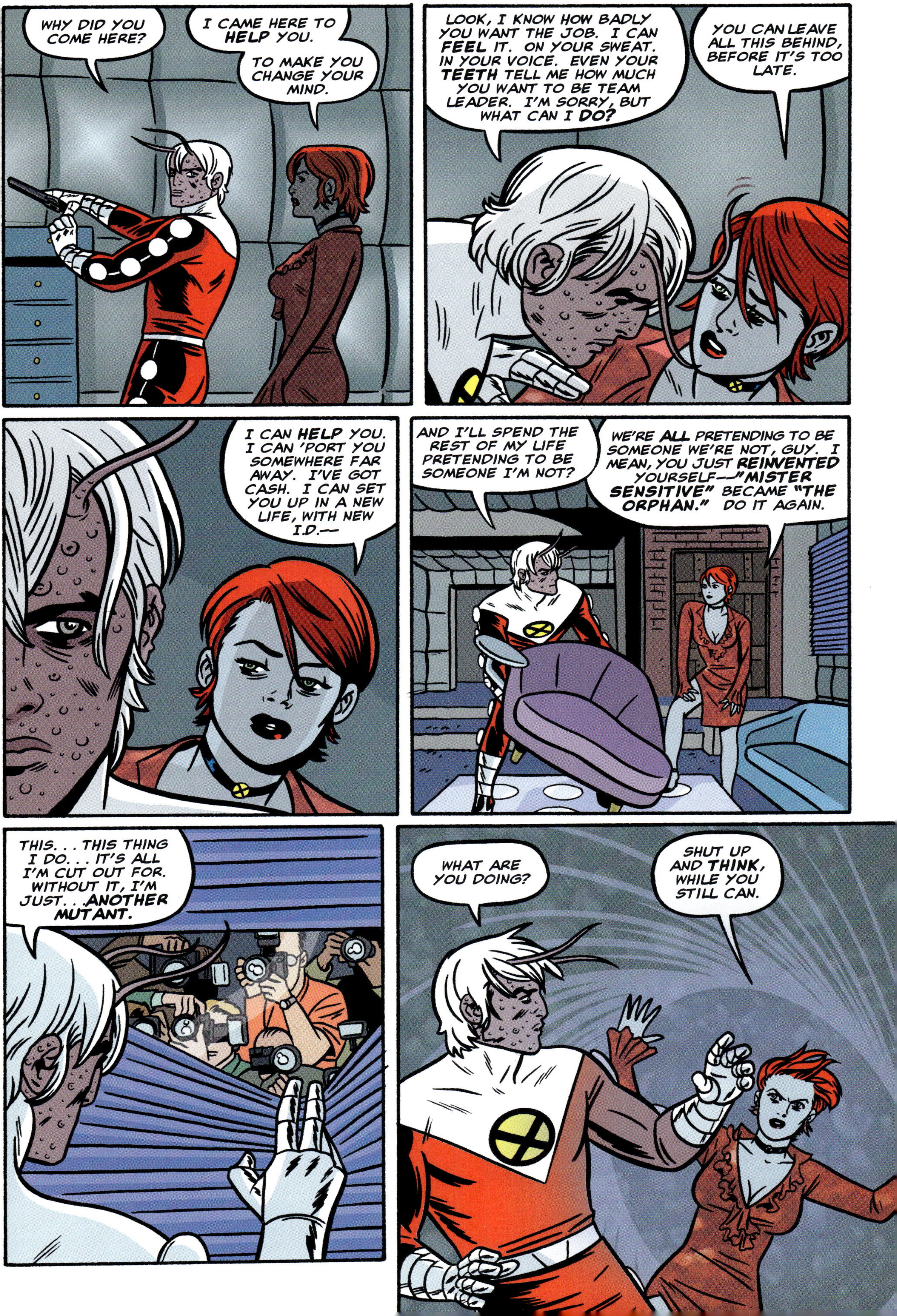

WHY DID YOU COME HERE?
I CAME HERE TO HELP YOU.
TO MAKE YOU CHANGE YOUR MIND.
LOOK, I KNOW HOW BADLY YOU WANT THE JOB. I CAN FEEL IT. ON YOUR SWEAT. IN YOUR VOICE. EVEN YOUR TEETH TELL ME HOW MUCH YOU WANT TO BE TEAM LEADER. I'M SORRY, BUT WHAT CAN I DO?
YOU CAN LEAVE ALL THIS BEHIND, BEFORE IT'S TOO LATE.
I CAN HELP YOU. I CAN 'PORT YOU SOMEWHERE FAR AWAY. I'VE GOT CASH. I CAN SET YOU UP IN A NEW LIFE, WITH NEW I.D.--
AND I'LL SPEND THE REST OF MY LIFE PRETENDING TO BE SOMEONE I'M NOT?
WE'RE ALL PRETENDING TO BE SOMEONE WE'RE NOT, GUY. I MEAN, YOU JUST REINVENTED YOURSELF--"MISTER SENSITIVE" BECAME "THE ORPHAN." DO IT AGAIN.
THIS... THIS THING I DO... IT'S ALL I'M CUT OUT FOR. WITHOUT IT, I'M JUST... ANOTHER MUTANT.
WHAT ARE YOU DOING?
SHUT UP AND THINK, WHILE YOU STILL CAN.

STAN LEE PRESENTS
PETER MILLIGAN-WRITER
M.D. "DOC" ALLRED-ARTIST
AND THEN THERE WERE SIX
LAURA ALLRED-COLORS AND SEPS
JOHN MIESEGAES-ASSISTANT EDITOR
JOE QUESADA-EDITOR IN CHIEF
MIKE ALLRED & BLAMBOT-LETTERS
AXEL ALONSO-EDITOR
BILL JEMAS-PRESIDENT
TAKE A LOOK, GUY SMITH, OR MISTER SENSITIVE, OR THE ORPHAN, OR WHATEVER YOU WANT TO CALL YOURSELF--IT'S A LONG WAY DOWN.
DO YOU HAVE A HEAD FOR HEIGHTS?

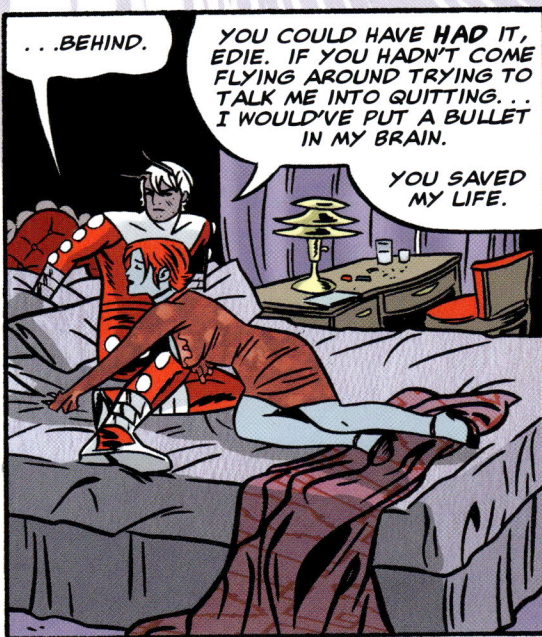

DIEGO ARDILLES. YOUR CONTACT IN **BASTRONA.** HE'S A SLEAZEBALL WHO'S DOING THIS FOR THE MONEY. ONCE HE'S FULFILLED HIS PURPOSE, HIS SAFETY IS NOT A PRIORITY.

YOUR **ONE** PRIORITY IS TO RESCUE **PACO PEREZ.**

IF WHAT DIEGO SAYS IS TRUE, THEY'RE DOING ALL KINDS OF SCARY STUFF TO THE LITTLE GUY, TRYING TO TEST AND HARNESS WHAT POWERS HE HAS.

EXCUSE ME. WE'RE GOING INTO A HOSTILE COUNTRY ON THE WORD OF A CHARACTER WHO **SELLS** INFORMATION. ISN'T THAT A LITTLE... **INCAUTIOUS?**

MYLES, IT'S PROBABLY **SUICIDALLY** INCAUTIOUS. BUT YOU DON'T GIVE A DAMN ABOUT THAT BECAUSE YOU'RE X-FORCE.

I SEE. THANK YOU.

D'OH!

IT GOES WITHOUT SAYING THAT THE MISSION IS UNOFFICIAL. **TRY** NOT TO GET CAUGHT.

SO, EDIE. HEARD YOU WERE GONNA HEAD UP A SPLINTER GROUP.

MEDIA "B.S." I'LL STICK AROUND. WITH **OUR** MORTALITY RATE, THERE'S **ALWAYS** THE CHANCE OF A QUICK PROMOTION.

SOMEONE'S MOVING AROUND! I TOLD YOU ALL NOT TO MOVE AROUND!

I . . . I'M HAVING TROUBLE STOPPING MYSELF EXPANDING.

THE PEOPLE'S REPUBLIC OF BASTRONA.

WELL GO ON A DAMN DIET, OR NEXT TIME YOU CAN CATCH A PLANE.

YOU OKAY? YOU LOOK BEAT.

IT'S THAT TIME OF THE MONTH. MAKES 'PORTING A REAL EFFORT. I COULD TAKE ANOTHER AMPOULE, BUT I DON'T WANT TO GET TOO CRANKY.

I MIGHT BE ABLE TO REVITALIZE YOU. DO YOU MIND IF I PUT MY HANDS ON YOUR SCALP?

HEY, IF YOU DON'T MIND GETTING HAIR GEL UNDER YOUR FINGER-NAILS.

QUITE FASCINATING IMAGERY. INDIGENOUS SPIRIT WORSHIP... UNRECONSTRUCTED SOCIALISM... HALF-REMEMBERED CATHOLICISM.

AND SOME A DEM CHICKENS CAN REALLY SHAKE IT.

NOT TO MENTION THE ROOSTERS.

WAIT FOR ME HERE.

YOU'RE NOT GOING DOWN THERE ON YOUR OWN?

I THOUGHT THAT WAS THE KIND OF THING TEAM LEADERS DID.

MAYBE IF I ACT LIKE ONE, I'LL START TO FEEL LIKE ONE.

DOOP, GET SOME SHOTS OF THE PARADE. IT'LL GIVE THE FILM SOMETHING INTERESTING TO CUT AWAY TO.

LISTEN TO YOU, MR. SODERBERGH!

ALL NEW RECRUITS HAVE TO ATTEND COURSES ON COMMUNICATION, MEDIA AND THE X-GENERATION.

SPTAKATAKATAK

I SHOULDN'T EVEN BE HERE.

I'M DEAD.

SORRY, MISTER. NOTHING PERSONAL.

WHERE THE HELL IS HE?

DIEGO. . .

OR I SHOULD BE, BY THE RULES OF MY GAME.

NOW YOU'VE GOT A REALLY GOOD REASON TO BE NERVOUS.

WHAT DOES THAT MAKE ME? A CHEAT?

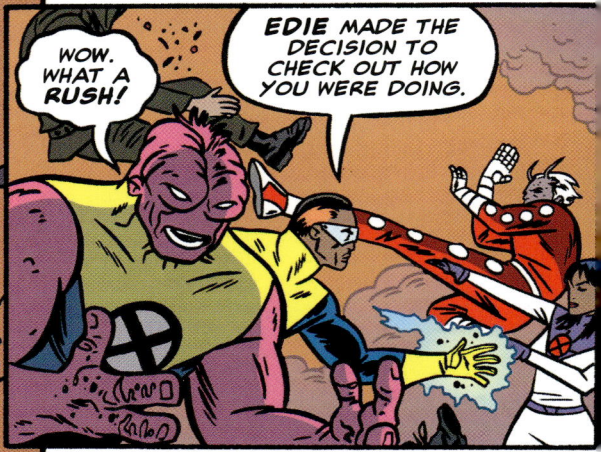

FUNNY. . .IT FEELS LIKE . . . IT SHOULD **HURT** MORE THAN THIS.

SAINT ANNA'S GONNA TAKE CARE OF YOU TILL WE GET YOU FIXED UP, BROTHER.

I'M WAY BEYOND **FIXING**, BILLY BOB.

ANYWAY. . .ONE LESS OF **MY KIND** TO WORRY ABOUT, RIGHT?

YEAH. RIGHT.

AND THEN THERE WERE SIX.

LEAVE IT, EDIE.

HEY, GUY! ORPHAN BOY! KEEP THIS UP, AND THERE'LL BE NO TEAM LEFT FOR YOU TO **LEAD**.

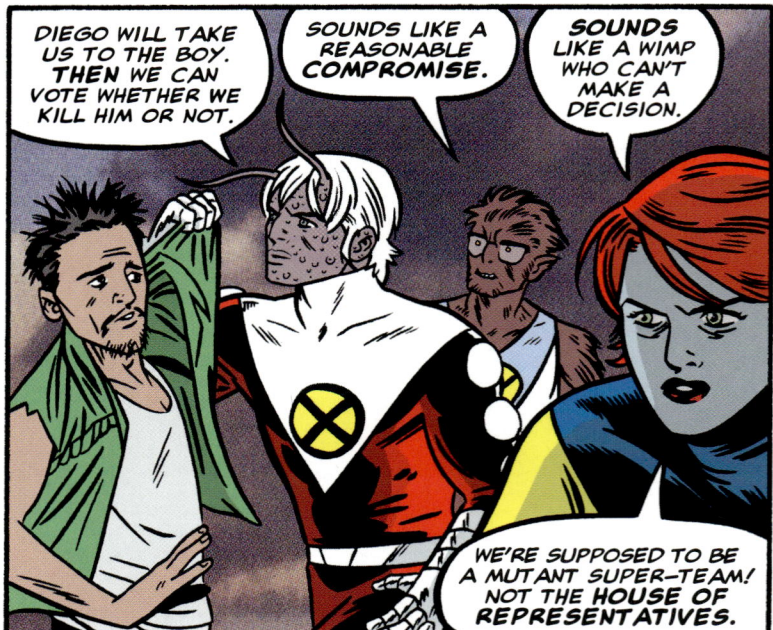

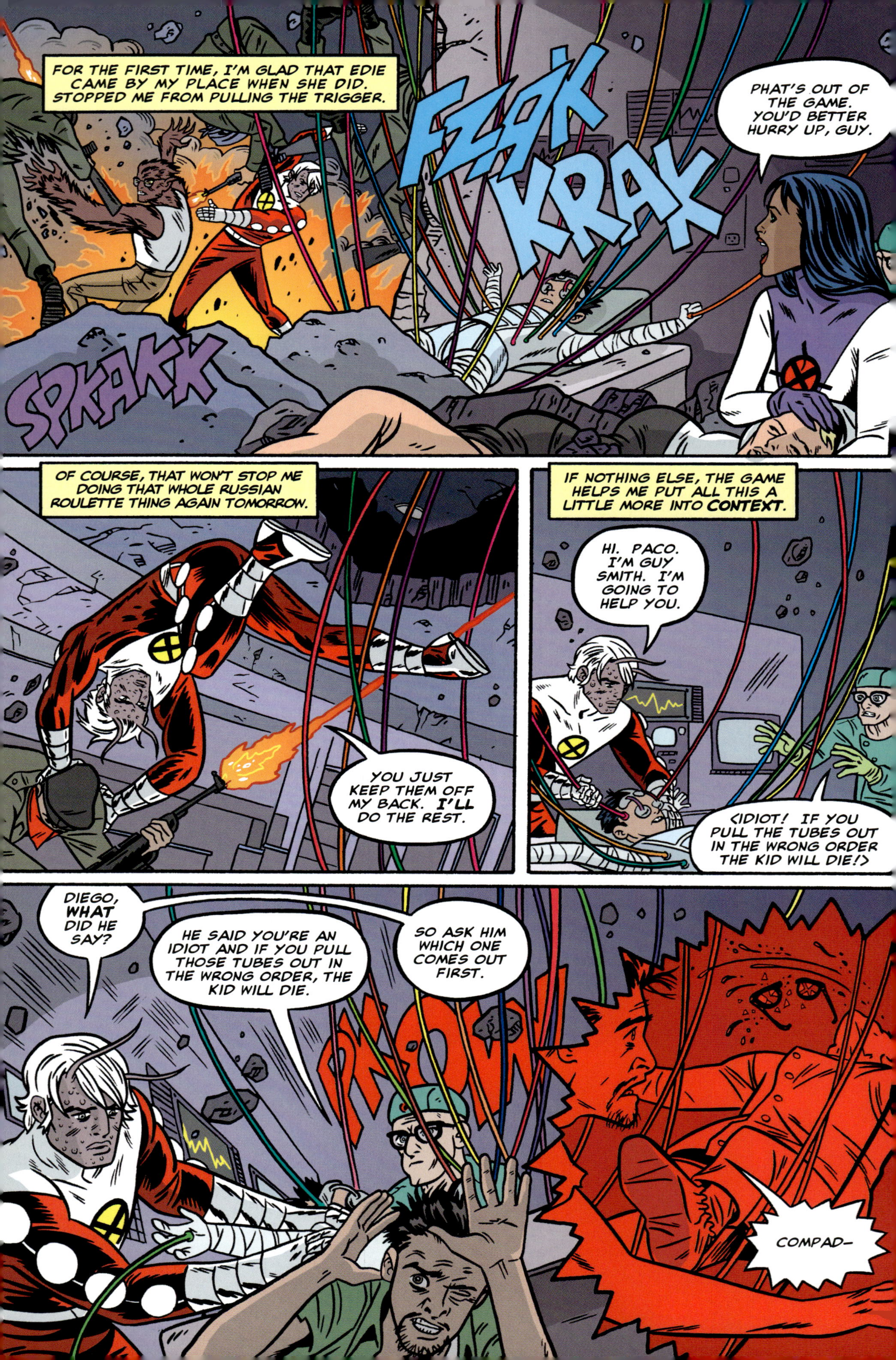
FOR THE FIRST TIME, I'M GLAD THAT EDIE CAME BY MY PLACE WHEN SHE DID. STOPPED ME FROM PULLING THE TRIGGER.
FZAK
KRAK
PHAT'S OUT OF THE GAME. YOU'D BETTER HURRY UP, GUY.
SPKAKK
OF COURSE, THAT WON'T STOP ME DOING THAT WHOLE RUSSIAN ROULETTE THING AGAIN TOMORROW.
YOU JUST KEEP THEM OFF MY BACK. I'LL DO THE REST.
IF NOTHING ELSE, THE GAME HELPS ME PUT ALL THIS A LITTLE MORE INTO CONTEXT.
HI. PACO. I'M GUY SMITH. I'M GOING TO HELP YOU.
<IDIOT! IF YOU PULL THE TUBES OUT IN THE WRONG ORDER THE KID WILL DIE!>
DIEGO, WHAT DID HE SAY?
HE SAID YOU'RE AN IDIOT AND IF YOU PULL THOSE TUBES OUT IN THE WRONG ORDER, THE KID WILL DIE.
SO ASK HIM WHICH ONE COMES OUT FIRST.
COMPAD-

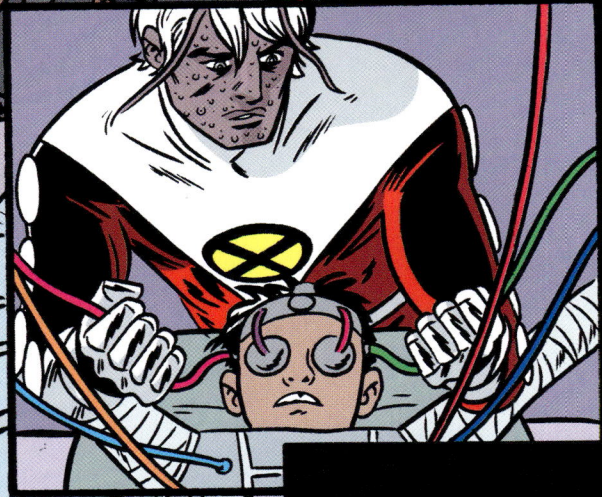

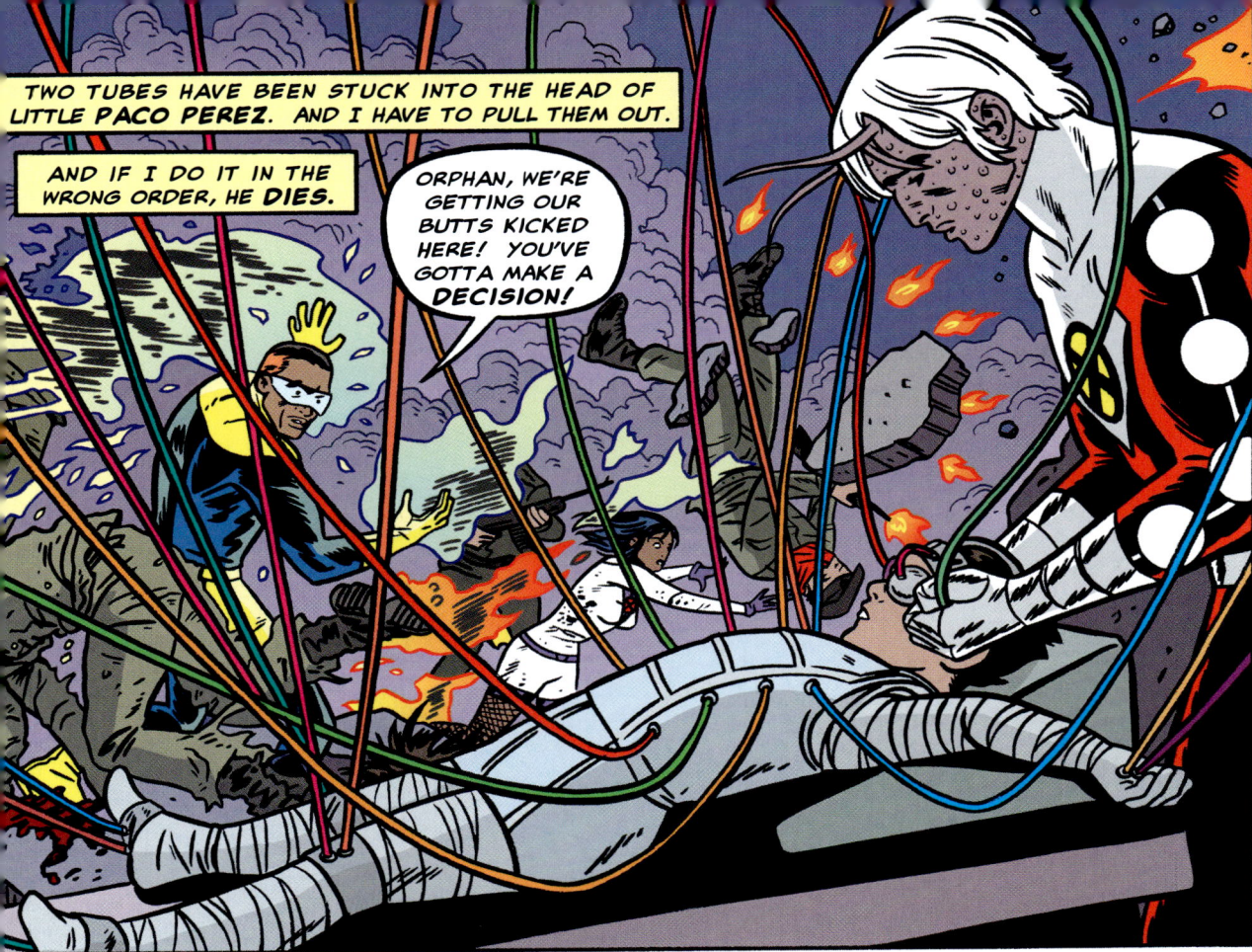

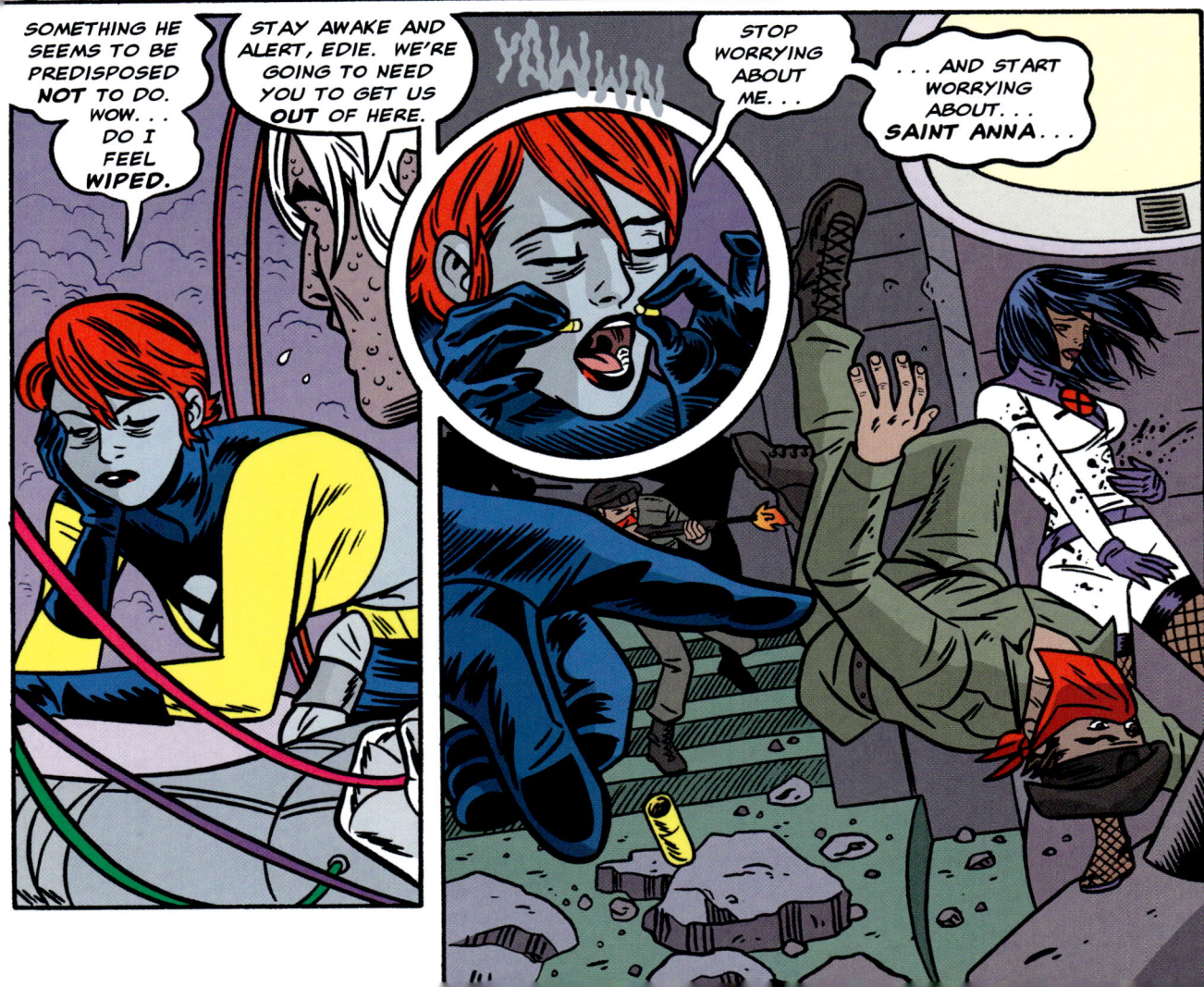

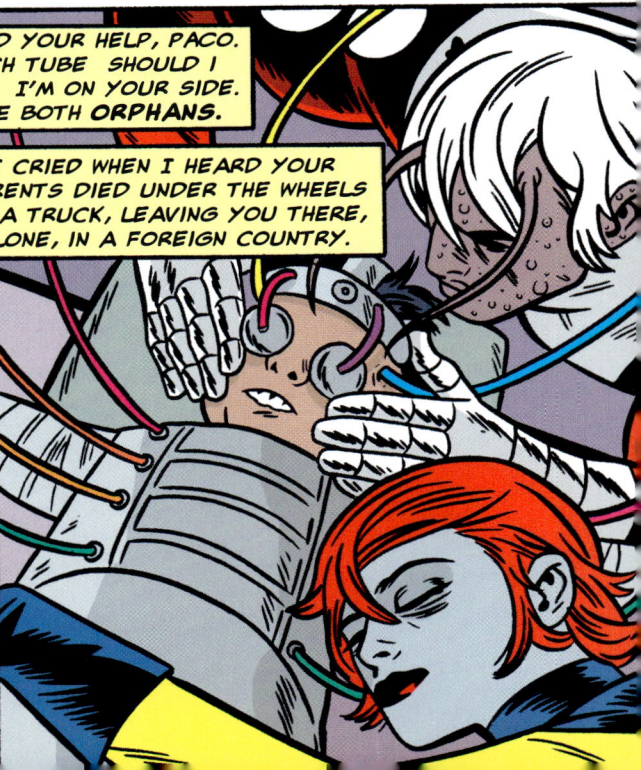

IT'S NO GOOD. CAN'T FEEL **DEEP** ENOUGH.

BUT THERE ARE TIMES WHEN YOU'VE JUST **GOT** TO HURT.

THIS WON'T TAKE LONG, I PROMISE.

DANG, GUY! WHAT THE—

AND YOU HAVE MY PERMISSION TO AVERT YOUR EYES.

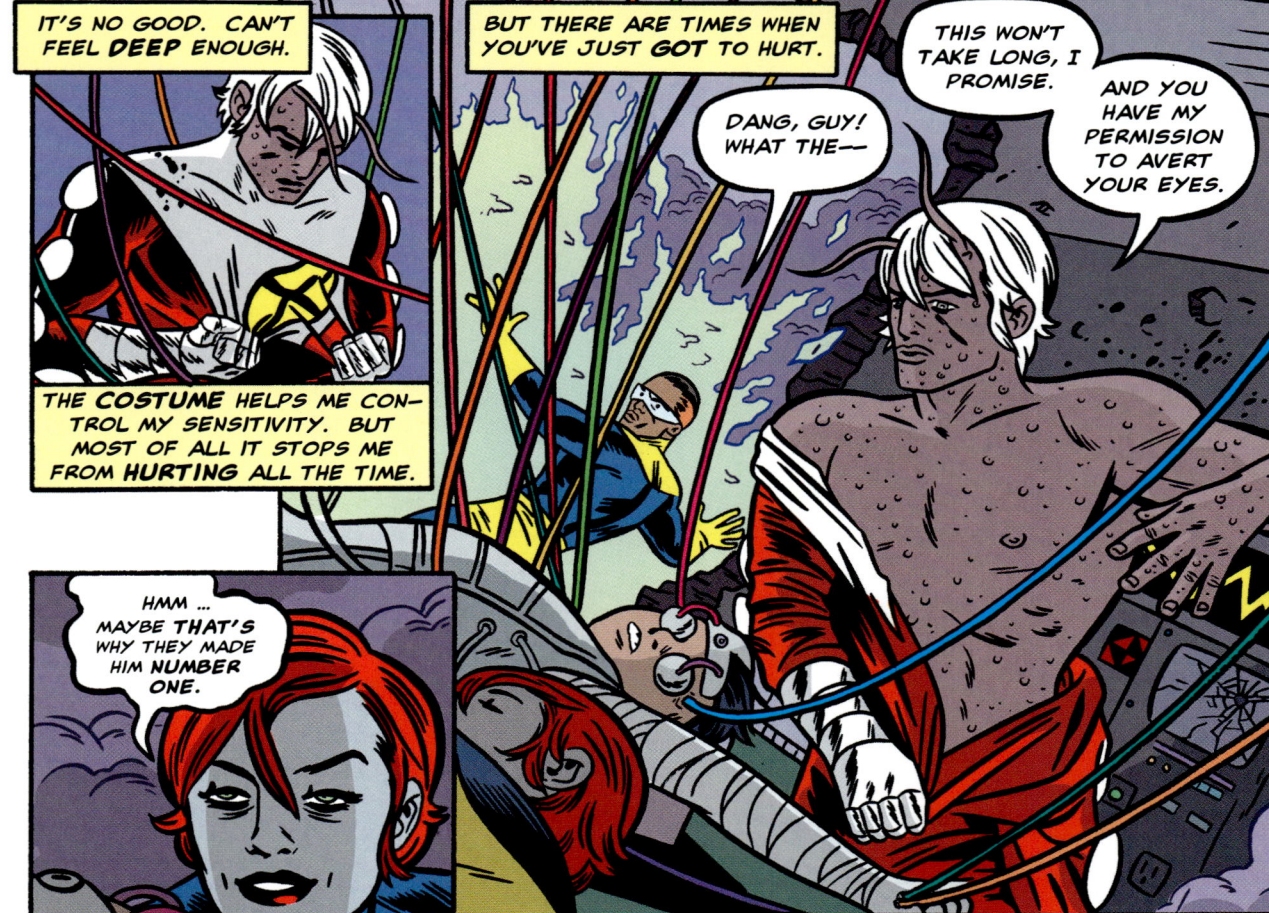

THE **COSTUME** HELPS ME CONTROL MY SENSITIVITY. BUT MOST OF ALL IT STOPS ME FROM **HURTING** ALL THE TIME.

HMM ... MAYBE **THAT'S** WHY THEY MADE HIM **NUMBER ONE.**

SORRY, **DOOP.** CAN'T RISK ANY OF THIS FOOTAGE FINDING ITS WAY TO THE **NATIONAL ENQUIRER.**

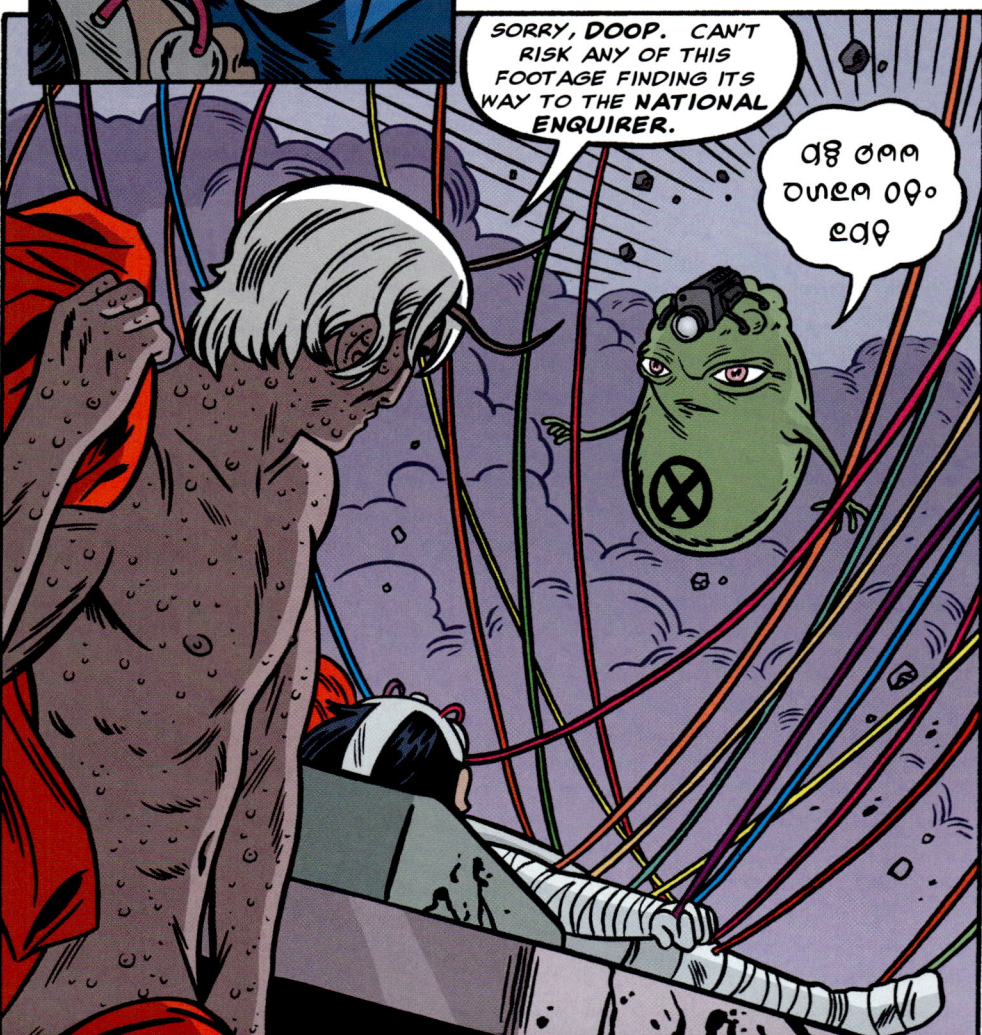

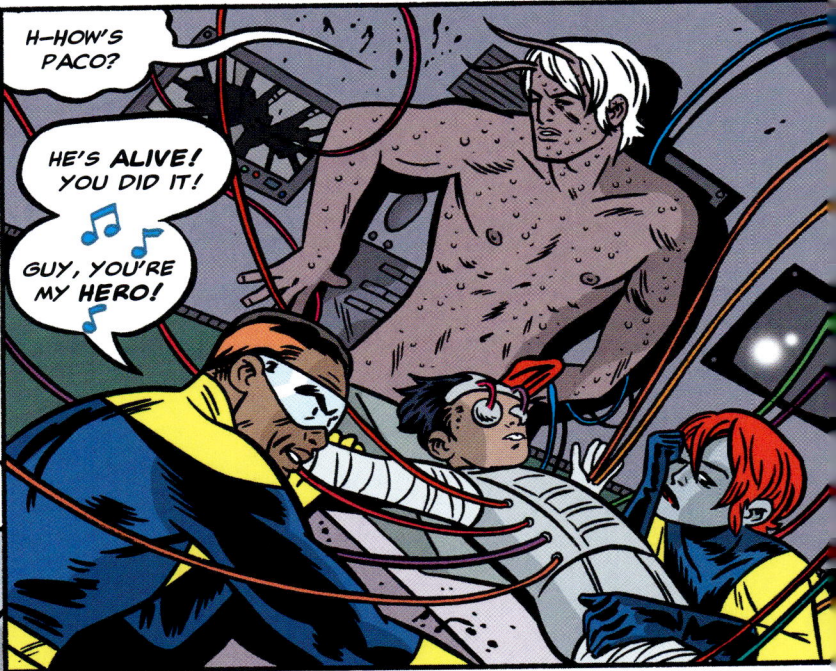

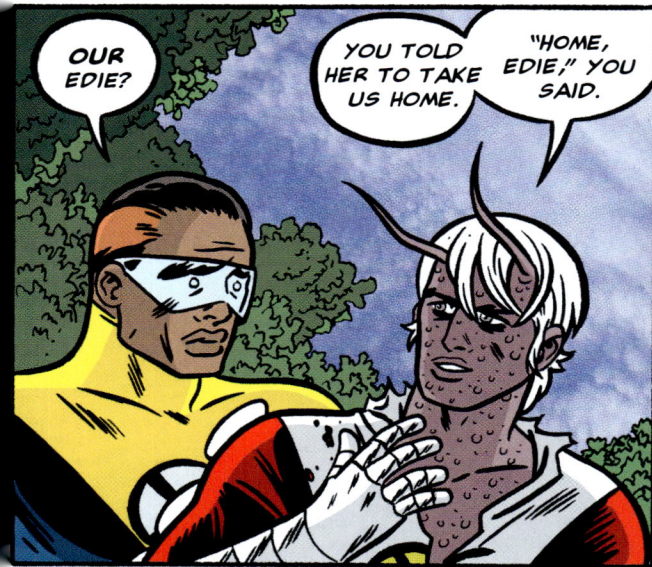

THIS IS **CHANNEL X** WISHING EDIE SAWYER—AKA U-GO GIRL—THE BEST OF LUCK IN HER BATTLE AGAINST WHAT MIGHT JUST BE THE TOUGHEST ADVERSARY SHE'LL EVER FACE.

SAWYER HAS JUST CHECKED INTO THE EXCLUSIVE PAT DOWNEY CLINIC, WHERE SHE'LL RECEIVE A LITTLE PROFESSIONAL HELP IN HER COURAGEOUS STRUGGLE WITH——

PAIN KILLERS AND ALCOHOL?

WE THOUGHT IT STRUCK THE RIGHT BALANCE BETWEEN **PATHOS** AND **SELF-ABUSE**.

WE DON'T WANT OUR ENEMIES KNOWING THAT EDIE'S OVER-RELIANCE ON HER LITTLE PICK-ME-UPS HAS TEMPORARILY SCREWED UP HER ABILITY TO ACCURATELY **TELEPORT**.

OUR **ENEMIES**? YOU MEAN LIKE THE FORMER MEMBERS OF **X-FORCE**?

I **MEAN** SUPER-VILLAINS. TYRANTS. EVIL GENIUSES. AND, NOW THAT WE'RE ON THE SUBJECT, **COMMUNIST REGIMES**.

WHERE **IS** HE, GUY?

HE'S **SAFE**.

I DIDN'T EXPECT HIM TO BE HANGING BY HIS FINGERNAILS FROM A TALL BUILDING.

WHERE IS HE?

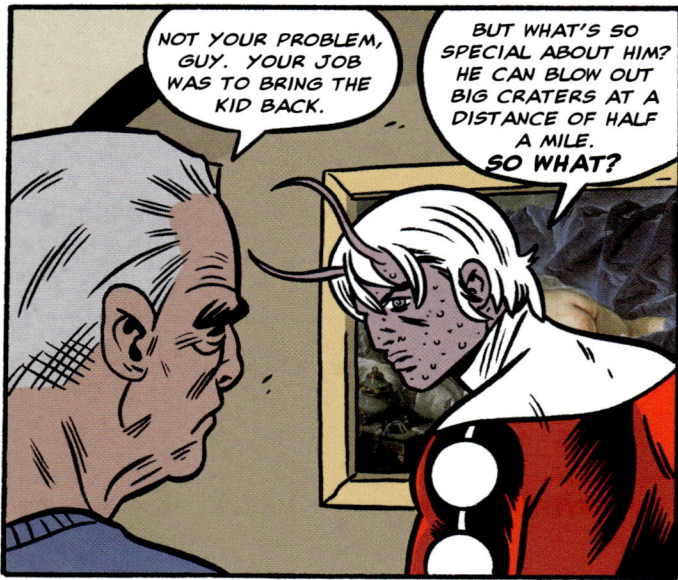

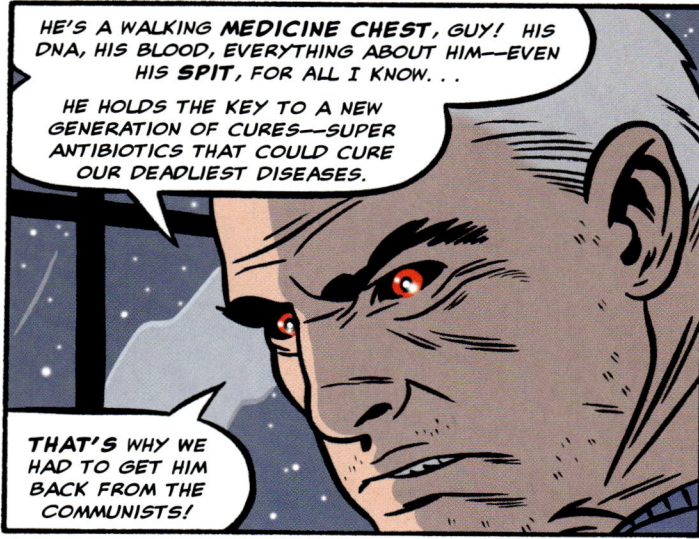

I FEEL SOMETHING LEAVING ME... A SUDDEN EMPTY HOLE INTO WHICH MY SELF QUICKLY RUSHES IN.
HE STANDS THERE WITH A SMILE ON HIS FACE AS HIS DAUGHTER'S ASHES MELT AROUND HIM.
IT'S FIVE MINUTES BEFORE HE CAN SPEAK.
I SAW HER! I SAW MY DAUGHTER. BEING BORN, GROWING UP. SO MUCH. . .I KNOW HER, SENOR SMITH! I HAVE MEMORIES OF HER. . .MEMORIES OF THINGS AND PLACES THAT I HAVE NEVER EXPERIENCED. . .
THANK YOU! HOW CAN I EVER REPAY YOU FOR THIS. . . FOR THIS GIFT?
IT WAS SAINT ANNA'S GIFT, NOT MINE. THOUGH THERE IS SOMETHING YOU CAN DO FOR ME.
IF IT'S IN MY POWER, I WILL DO IT.
HIS NAME IS PACO. HE SPEAKS SPANISH BUT HASN'T SPOKEN A WORD SINCE SOME VERY BAD THINGS HAPPENED TO HIM. HE NEEDS A HOME. HE NEEDS A NEW NAME. A NEW FAMILY.
HE NEEDS LOVE.
WE ALL NEED THAT, MISTER SMITH.

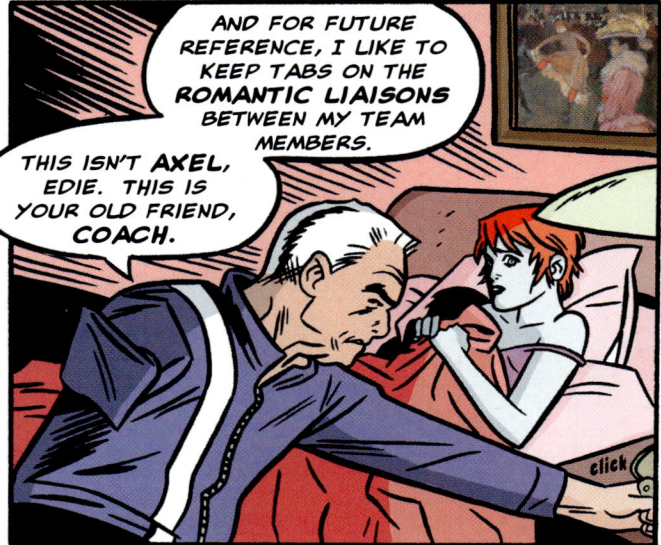

HOW WAS THAT?

NOT REALLY SURE IF I FOUND, YOU KNOW, MY "CENTER."

AND YOU KNOW MY CONDITIONS: BEFORE I GIVE FINAL PERMISSION FOR YOU TO USE ME IN YOUR "DOOP'S-EYE VIDEO OF THE NEW X-FORCE'S FIRST YEAR"...

I DON'T CARE HOW LONG WE'VE KNOWN EACH OTHER, I REALLY DON'T KNOW WHY YOU'RE STILL HANGIN' WITH THESE CLOWNS!

EASY FOR YOU TO SAY.

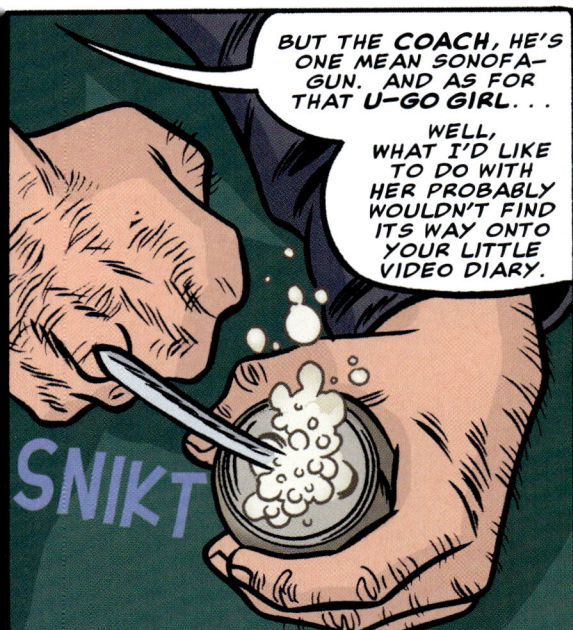

BUT THE COACH, HE'S ONE MEAN SONOFA-GUN. AND AS FOR THAT U-GO GIRL...

WELL, WHAT I'D LIKE TO DO WITH HER PROBABLY WOULDN'T FIND ITS WAY ONTO YOUR LITTLE VIDEO DIARY.

SNIKT

YA MEAN...?

WE'RE
CLOSED
I DON'T KNOW, DOOP. EVEN FOR AN OLD FRIEND, YOU'RE ASKIN' A HELLUVA LOT.
STAN LEE PRESENTS
X-FORCE: SNIKT!
PETER MILLIGAN-WRITER
MICHAEL ALLRED-ARTIST
LAURA ALLRED-COLORIST
DOC ALLRED & BLAMBOT-LETTERS
JOHN MIESEGAES-ASST. EDITOR
AXEL ALONSO-EDITOR
JOE QUESADA-CHIEF
BILL JEMAS-PRESIDENT
X-FORCE
CAFE'
AN' I GOT A FEELING THAT THE NEXT FEW DAYS COULD GET KINDA MESSY FOR YOUR NEW CREW.

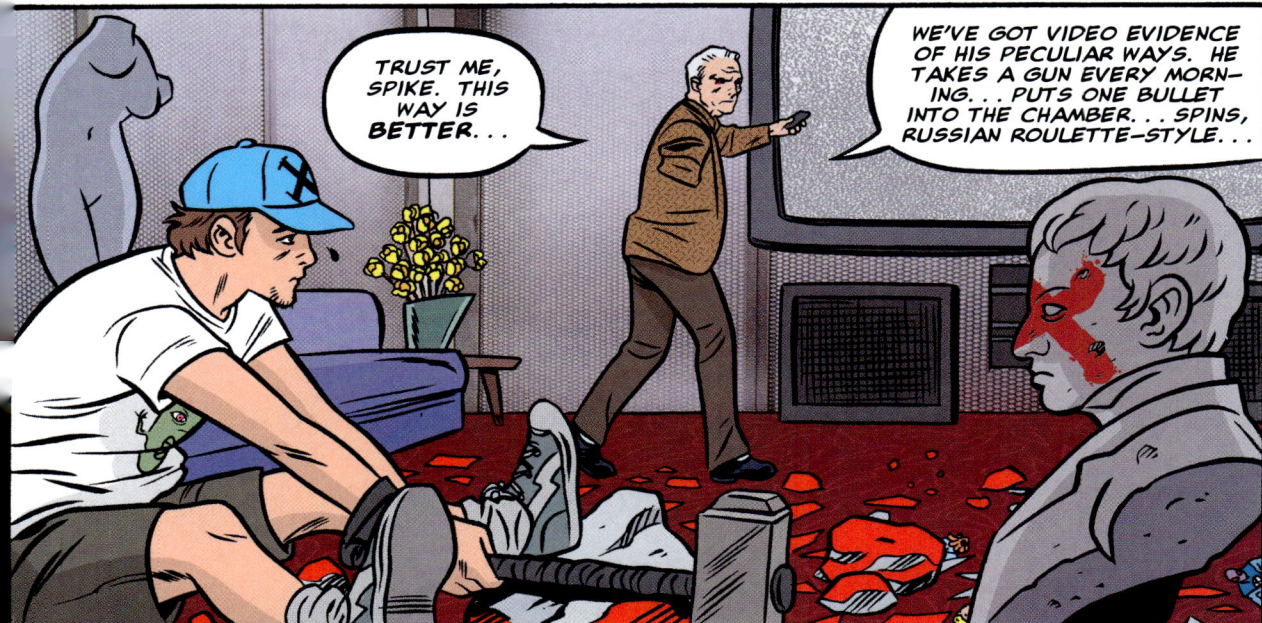

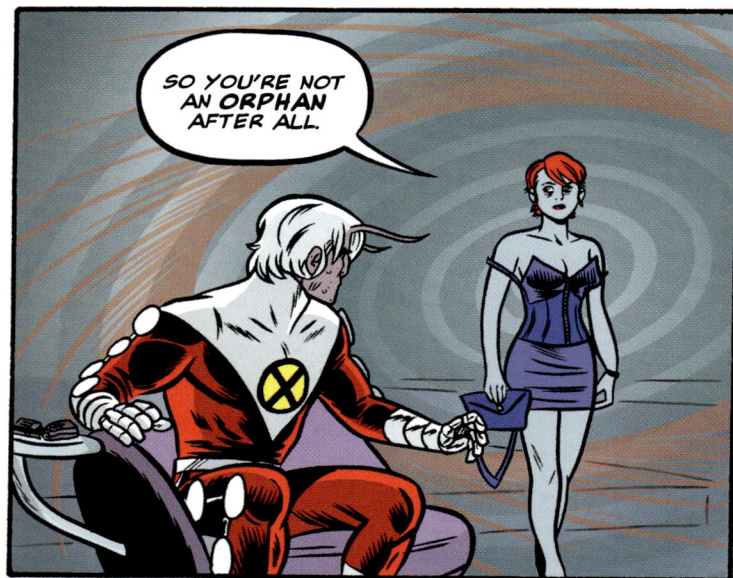

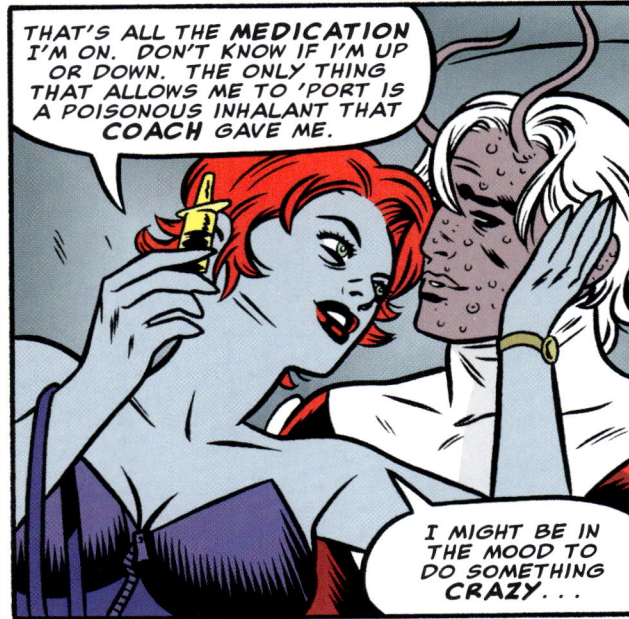

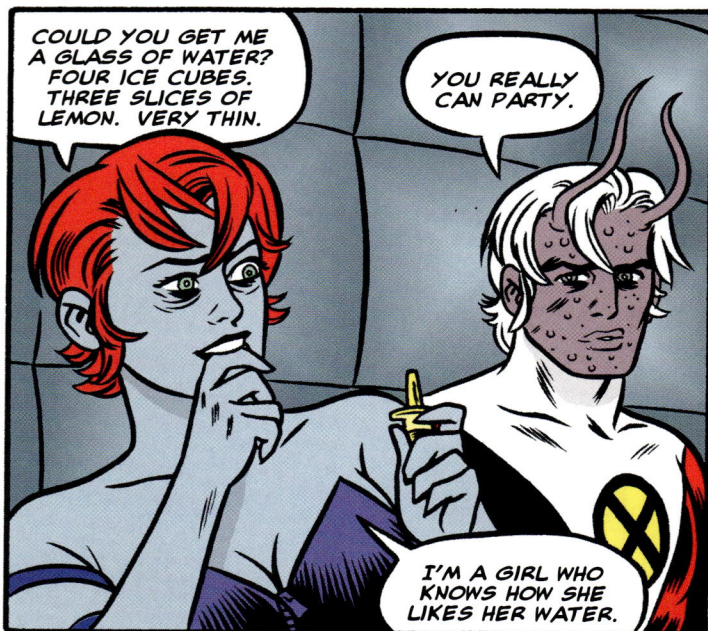

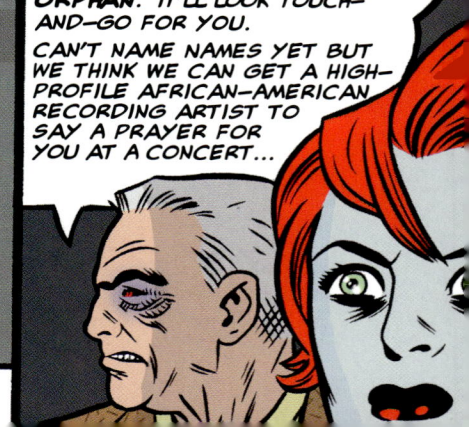

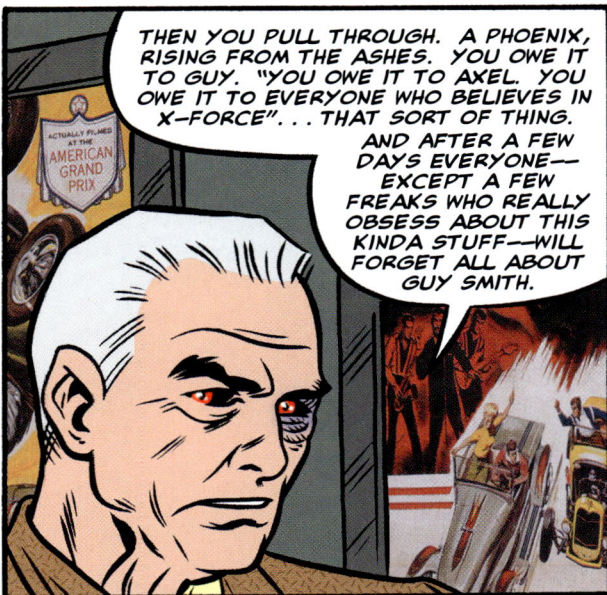

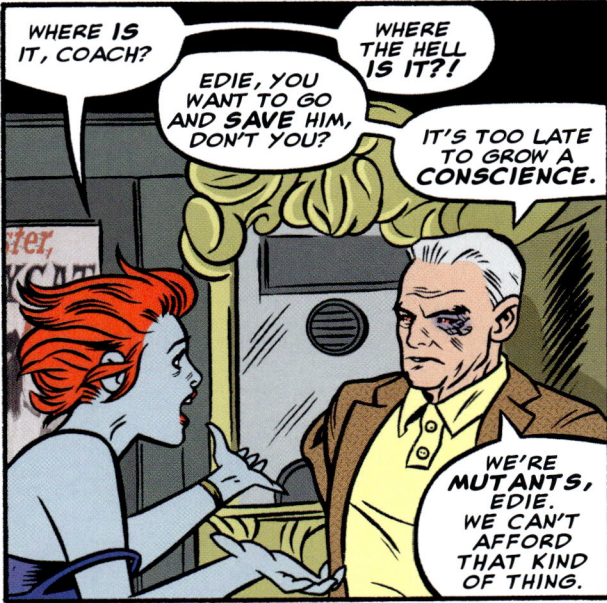

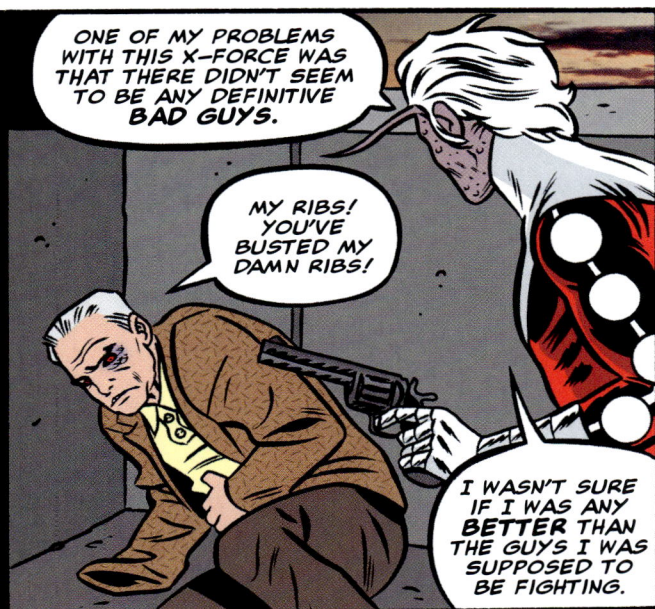

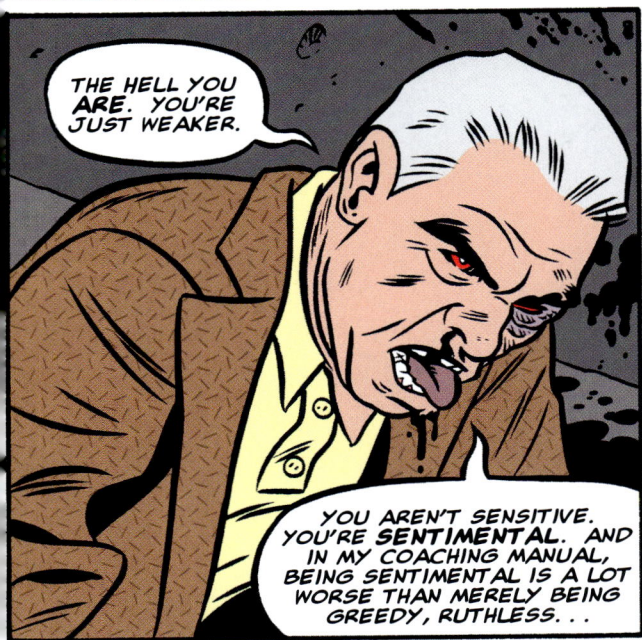

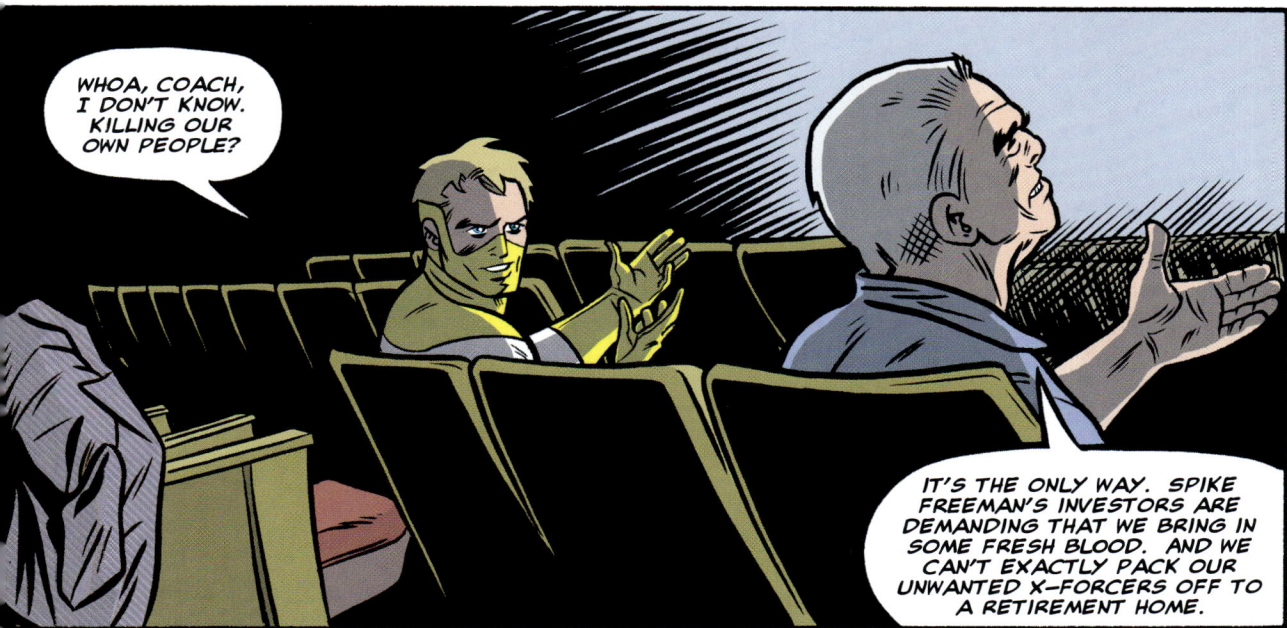

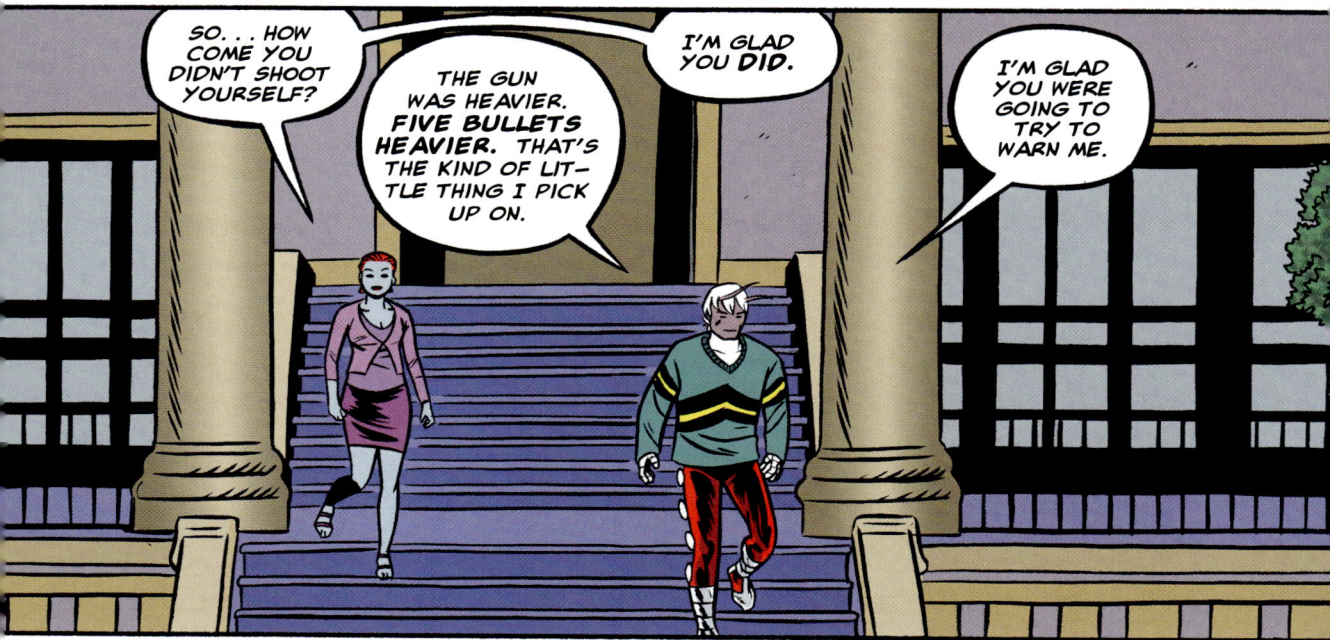

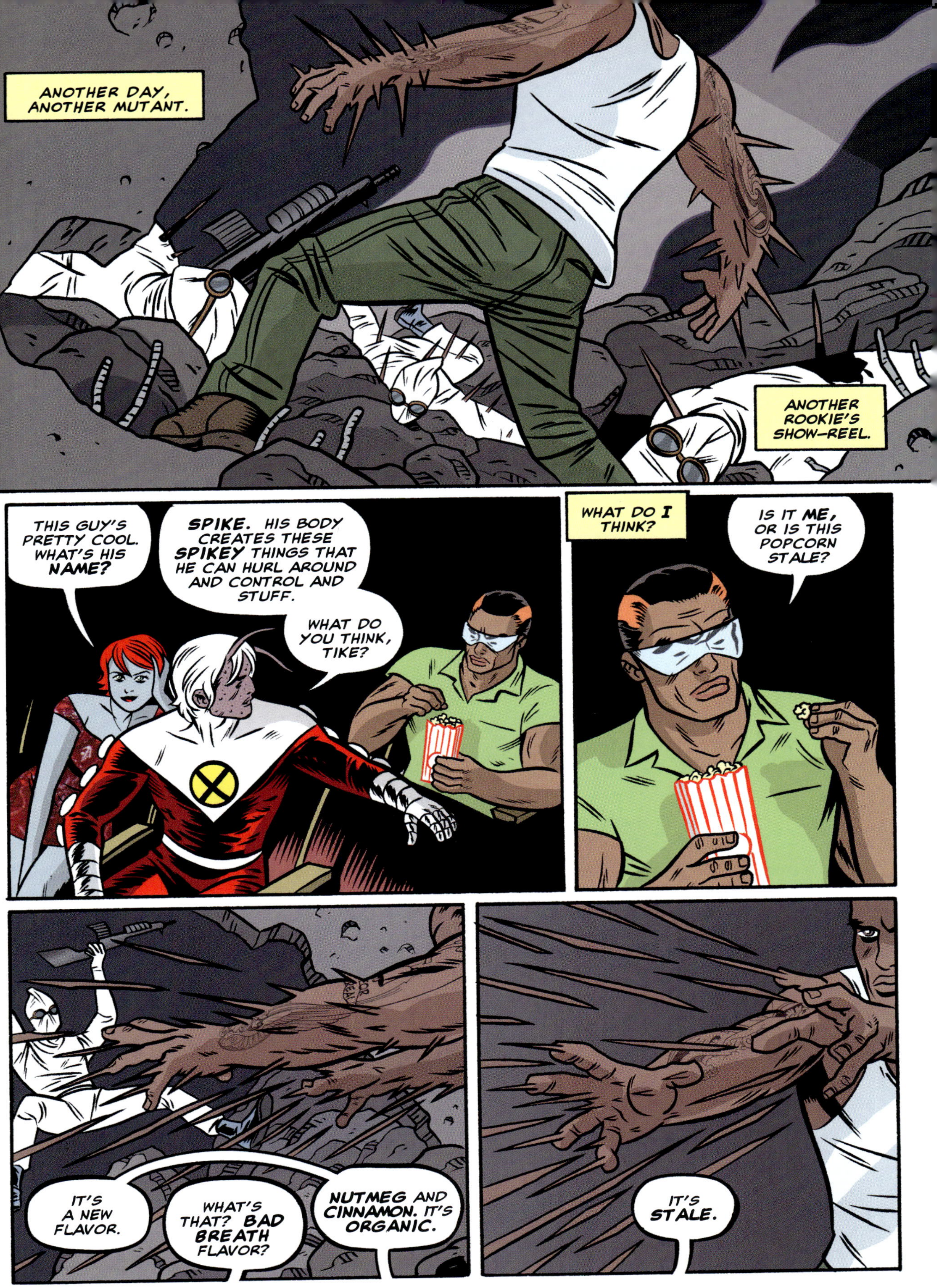
ANOTHER DAY, ANOTHER MUTANT.
ANOTHER ROOKIE'S SHOW-REEL.
THIS GUY'S PRETTY COOL. WHAT'S HIS NAME?
SPIKE. HIS BODY CREATES THESE SPIKEY THINGS THAT HE CAN HURL AROUND AND CONTROL AND STUFF.
WHAT DO YOU THINK, TIKE?
WHAT DO I THINK?
IS IT ME, OR IS THIS POPCORN STALE?
IT'S A NEW FLAVOR.
WHAT'S THAT? BAD BREATH FLAVOR?
NUTMEG AND CINNAMON. IT'S ORGANIC.
IT'S STALE.

STAN LEE PRESENTS

LACUNA:
PART ONE: CAPTAIN COCONUT

PETER MILLIGAN–WRITER   MICHAEL ALLRED–ARTIST

LAURA ALLRED– COLORIST   DOC ALLRED & BLAMBOT–LETTERS   JOHN MIESEGAES–ASST. EDITOR

AXEL ALONSO–EDITOR   JOE QUESADA–CHIEF   BILL JEMAS–PRESIDENT

WOW. HE COULD **SPIKE** ME ANY DAY OF THE WEEK.

EDIE, WE'RE NOT HERE TO DISCUSS YOUR LOVE LIFE.

HEY, DO I DETECT A LITTLE JEALOUSY?

DON'T BE RIDICULOUS.

WELL, TIKE? DO YOU THINK THE SPIKE IS X-FORCE MATERIAL?

ASK ME, HE AIN'T NOTHIN' BUT A GLORIFIED **SPEAR-CHUCKER.**

THEY'RE THE THREE **SENIOR** MEMBERS OF THE TEAM. WE'RE COOL ABOUT LETTIN' 'EM CHOOSE THE NEW GUYS.

BESIDES, THEY'VE MADE IT CLEAR THAT WE CAN HAVE A **VETO** OF ANY PROSPECTIVE MUTANTS. . .

AND YOU CHUMPS DON'T CARE THAT X-FORCE IS CURRENTLY KNOWN AS **GUY, TIKE, EDIE** AND THOSE **OTHER** TWO GUYS?

THAT'S AN EXAGGERATION.

YO! IS **THAT** WHAT THEY'RE **SAYING**?

TAKE MY ADVICE: THE MEDIA. MAKE 'EM NOTICE YOU. MAKE SOME **NOISE**.

HOW DO WE DO **THAT**?

TEAR IT UP SOME. MAKE IT LOOK LIKE IT'S **YOU GUYS** VERSUS THEM **OTHER** THREE. GIVE THE MARKETING BOYS SOMETHING TO SINK THEIR **TEETH** INTO.

YOU MEAN WE SHOULD. . . **PROVOKE** FIGHTS WITH OUR **TEAMMATES**?

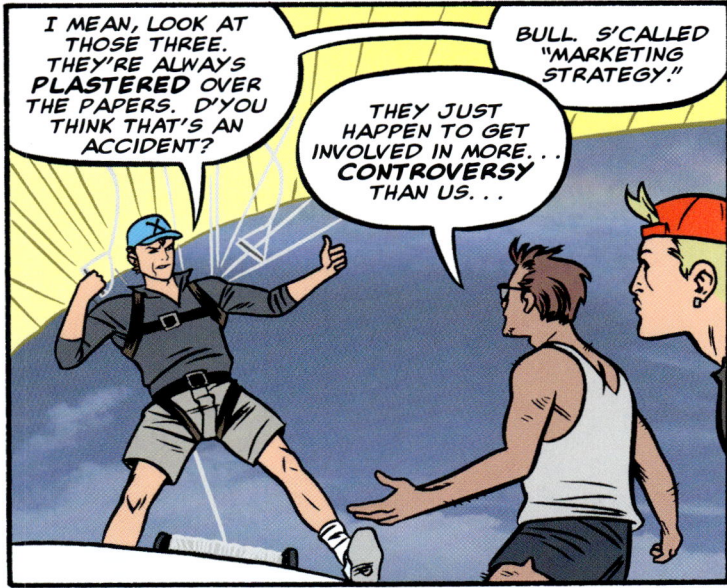

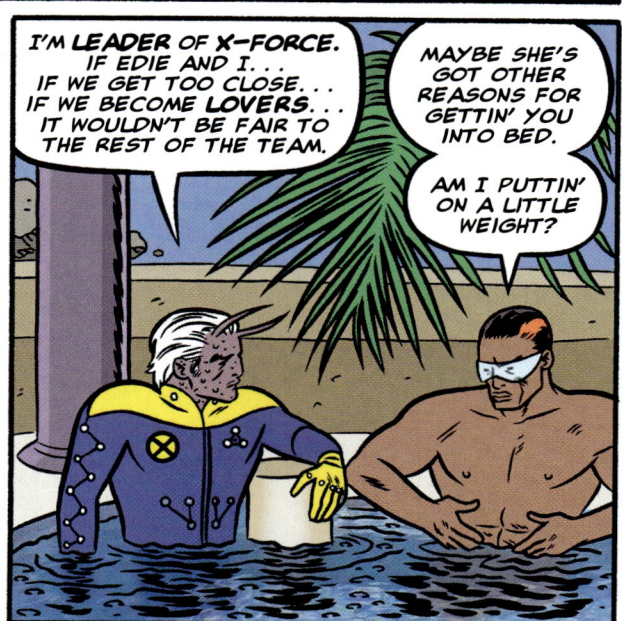

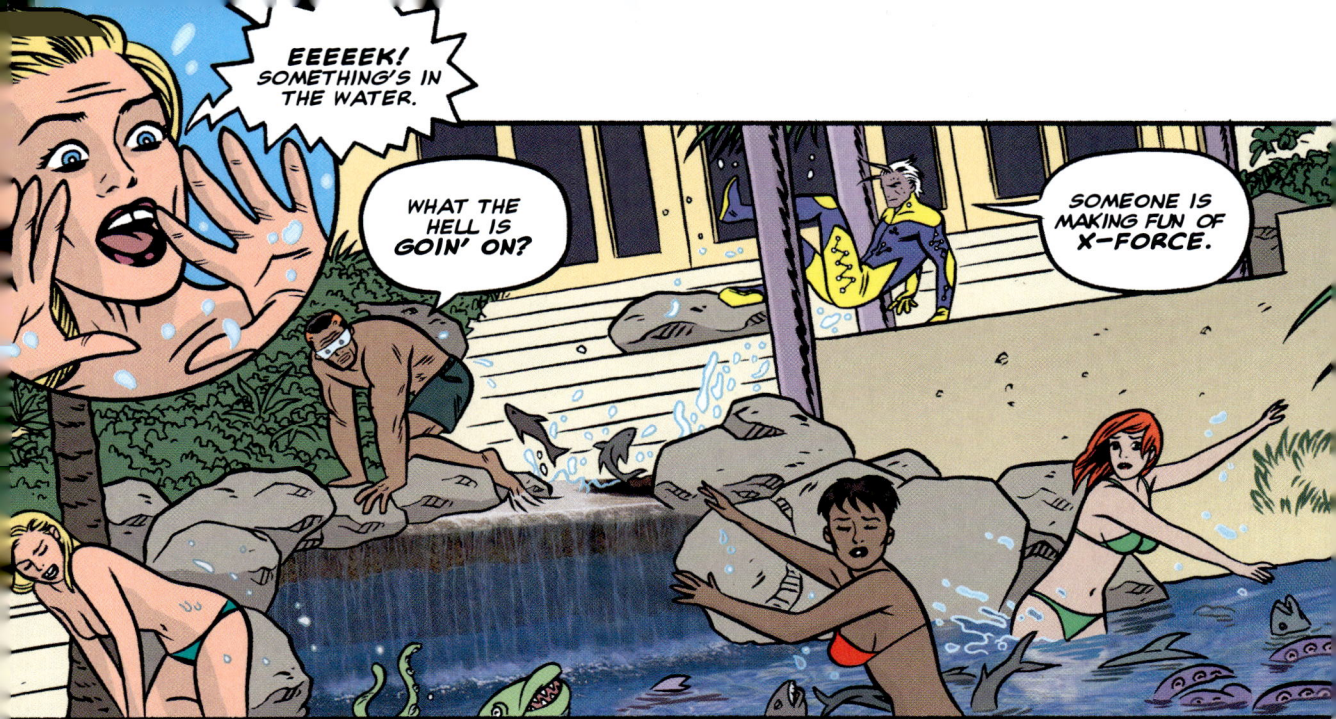

THIS WAS ONE OF MY MORE ENJOYABLE FIGHTS. MY UNDERWEAR WAS ITALIAN, MY PERFUME FRENCH, MY FIGHTING TACTICS. . .

. . . PURE YANKEE DOODLE.

EDIE, THIS IS REALLY TRASHY.

MUTE

IT'S JUST A PILOT FOR THE NETWORK. I'LL HAVE INPUT. IT'LL ACTUALLY BE A REAL INTERESTING INSIGHT INTO THE LIFE OF AN X-FORCE MUTANT.

FIGHTING TO KEEP THE WORLD FREE AND SAFE FOR UNBRIDLED PRODUCT PLACEMENT?

WHO KNOWS HOW LONG THIS GRAVY TRAIN IS GOING TO KEEP ROLLING? WE HAVE TO MAKE HAY WHILE THE MIXED METAPHORS LAST.

GUY, I KNOW THIS DESERTED BEACH IN MEXICO. WE COULD BE THERE NAKED QUICKER THAN YOU CAN SAY "MILLION DOLLAR TV CONTRACT."

WAIT! STOP PORTING, EDIE!

WHAT'S UP?

LET ME REPHRASE THAT...

I'D RATHER YOU DIDN'T REPHRASE ANYTHING. I... I DON'T THINK WE SHOULD DO THIS.

DO WHAT?

EMBARK UPON AN AFFAIR.

EAU DE X

AFFAIR? LIGHTEN UP, MR. SENSITIVE.

ALL I WAS TALKING ABOUT WAS HAVING SOME FUN. AFFAIR? SHEESH. THAT'S JUST SUCH A... NORM TERM.

YOU KNOW... BEING MUTANTS... MEANS WE CAN HAVE MUTANT MORALITY TOO. WE DON'T HAVE TO APE THE NORMS' WORN-OUT CODES OF CONDUCT. WE CAN MAKE OUR OWN RULES...

LACUNA

NO DECISION HAS BEEN MADE ABOUT WHO ARE GOING TO BE OUR NEXT TWO TEAM MEMBERS. LET'S SAY...

POX5

REPORT

LET'S SAY WE'RE STILL **EXPLORING** OUR **OPTIONS**.

THANK YOU, EDIE.

WHAT ABOUT **VENUS DEE MILO?**

GREAT MUTANT. PERFECT RECORD. NO COMMENT.

AND **DEAD GIRL?** SOME **LAS VEGAS HEAVY ROLLERS** ARE PUTTING A **LOT** A DOUGH ON HER GRAVE BEING **HOT.**

LET'S SAY **DEAD GIRL'S** CHANCES ARE STILL... **ALIVE** AND **KICKING.**

I'VE GOT A QUESTION... FOR **CAPTAIN COCONUT.**

WHO'S "CAPTAIN COCONUT"?

THE MUTANT FORMERLY KNOWN AS **THE ANARCHIST...**

...RENAMED BY THE **NATIONAL ASSOCIATION FOR KEEPING IT REAL** AS **CAPTAIN COCONUT.**

BECAUSE HE'S **BLACK** ON THE OUTSIDE.

AND **WHITE** ON THE INSIDE.

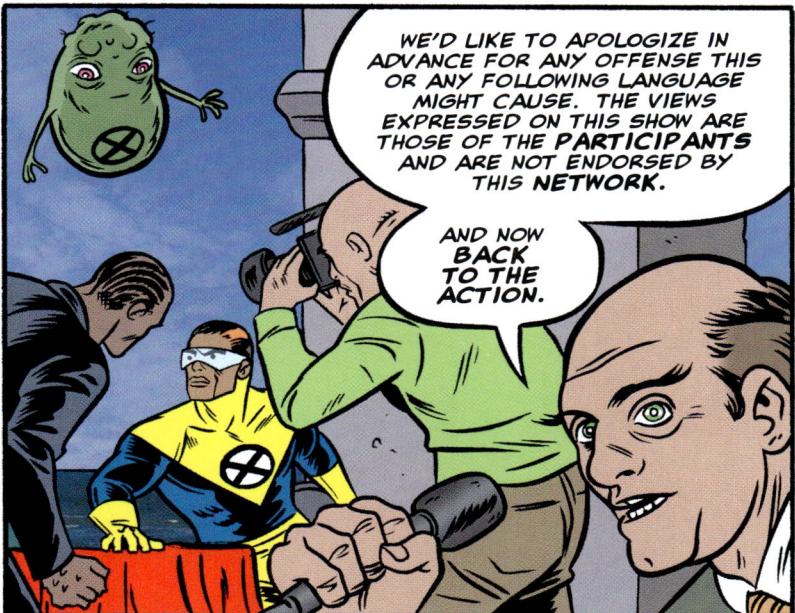

WHAT YOU WAITIN' FOR, CAP'N?

ONCE AGAIN, DRAMATIC EVENTS INTERRUPT AN X-FORCE PRESS CONFERENCE. HOW DO YOU **READ** THIS ONE, HEIDI?

I SUSPECT IT'S ALL **STAGED.** SPIKE'S PROFILE AND MARKETABILITY ARE RAISED. AND X-FORCE SEEMS MORE... POLITICALLY RELEVANT.

OF COURSE, THEY WILL AVOID DEALING WITH THE REAL ISSUES OF **RACE, GENDER** AND **CAPITAL** IN THIS COUNTRY.

THANKS, HEIDI—WHO, BY THE WAY, CHOSE TO DEFECT FROM COMMUNIST EAST GERMANY TO **THIS** COUNTRY...

THEY DON'T UNDERSTAND.

THEY DON'T GET WHAT X-FORCE IS **REALLY** ABOUT.

IT LOOKS LIKE TIKE AIN'T GONNA TAKE ANY MORE SMACK-TALK.

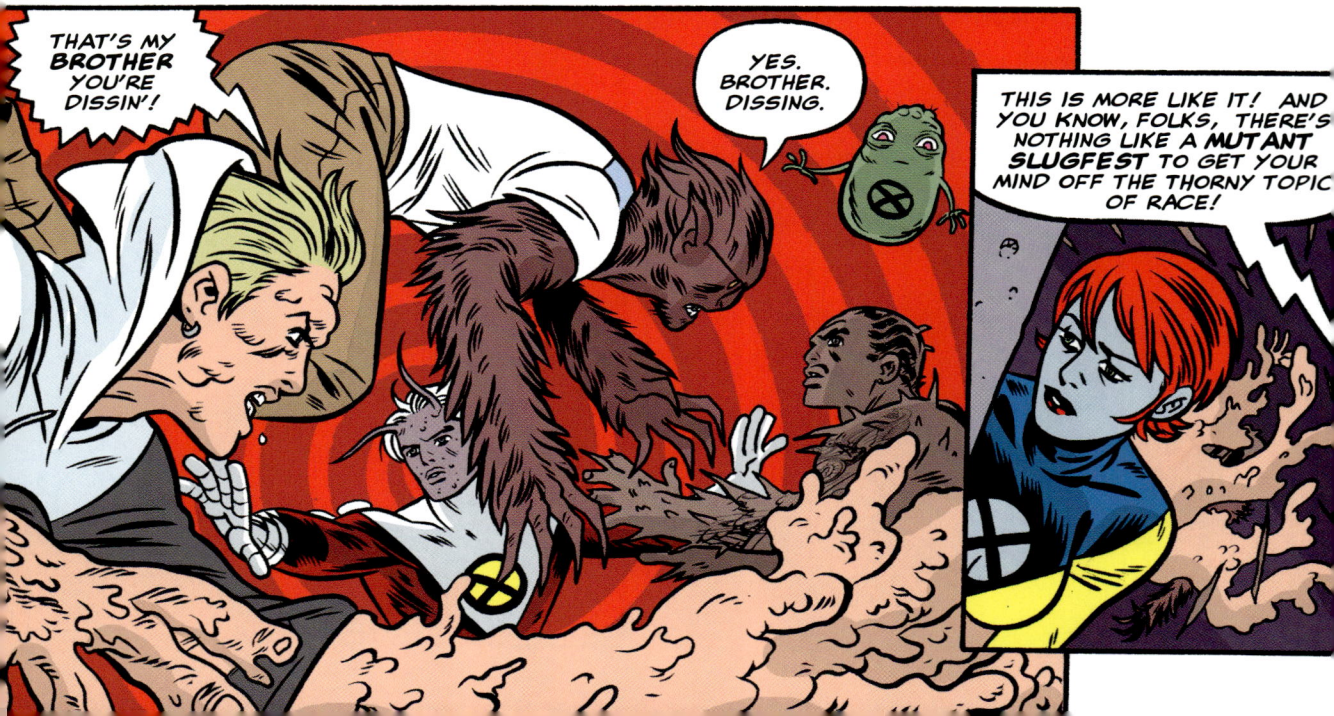

THAT WAS SPECTACULAR.

MAYBE I SHOULD HAVE DONE THAT TO SPIKE.

AS A GENERAL RULE, IT'S A GOOD THING NOT TO VAPORIZE PEOPLE. PARTICULARLY ON PRIME TIME TV...

A BEAT DOWN, THEN. TO PUT HIM IN HIS PLACE.

AND THEN EVERYONE WOULD HAVE THOUGHT THERE WAS SOMETHING IN WHAT HE SAID-- THAT YOU DIDN'T WANT HIM IN THE TEAM FOR PERSONAL REASONS.

AND THAT'S RIDICULOUS, RIGHT?

MAYBE.

RIGHT. RIDICULOUS.

THAT'S PRETTY IMPRESSIVE, AIN'T IT? I MEAN, ASK ME, HE LOOKS LIKE X-FORCE MATERIAL THROUGH AND THROUGH.

THAT'S NOT THE **POINT**, MR. FREEMAN.

CALL ME **SPIKE**.

AND IN CASE YOU WONDERED, I'M NOT KEEN ON HAVING THIS GUY AS PART OF THE TEAM JUST BECAUSE OUR NAMES ARE THE SAME.

THEN WHY **ARE** YOU SO KEEN? WE HAD AN AGREEMENT THAT TEAM SELECTION WOULD BE IN **OUR HANDS**.

I'M GETTING A LOT OF GRIEF OVER THIS. FROM A LOT OF INFLUENTIAL PEOPLE. WE CAN'T AFFORD TO HAVE X-FORCE SEEN AS A RACIST INSTITUTION.

WE AREN'T!

RIGHT, BUT YOU GOTTA BE **SEEN** NOT TO BE. THE DAYS WHEN A BIG CORPORATION COULD PUT A FEW BLACK PEOPLE ON RECEPTION AND CLAIM THEY WERE WORKING FOR A EGALITARIAN SOCIETY ARE LONG GONE.

LISTEN, **SPIKE**. WE RISK OUR LIVES IN THIS JOB. WE HAVE TO DEPEND ON THE GUY NEXT TO US.

THAT MEANS HE OR SHE HAS TO BE THE BEST, REGARDLESS OF COLOR, SEX, CREED **OR** MUTATION.

PERSONALLY, I THINK WE SHOULD BRING HIM IN. MAYBE FOR A **TRIAL PERIOD.**

THAT IS THE MOST HALF-ASSED THING I'VE EVER HEARD. **TRIAL PERIOD?** WE'RE CHOOSING A NEW TEAM MEMBER—NOT BUYING A **VACUUM CLEANER.**

IF YOU DON'T ME SAYING, YOU **DO** SEEM TO HAVE AN IRRATIONAL PROBLEM WITH THIS **SPIKE** CHARACTER.

I THINK TIKE'S RUNNING SCARED.

STICK TO YOUR **BOOKS,** MYLES.

AND PHAT, I MIGHT GIVE A DAMN ABOUT WHAT YOU THINK—**WHEN YOU STOP BEING A WHITE BOY** WHO WISHES HE WAS **BLACK.**

OR WHEN **YOU** STOP BEING A **BLACK** MAN WHO WISHES HE WAS **WHITE.**

TOUCHÉ.

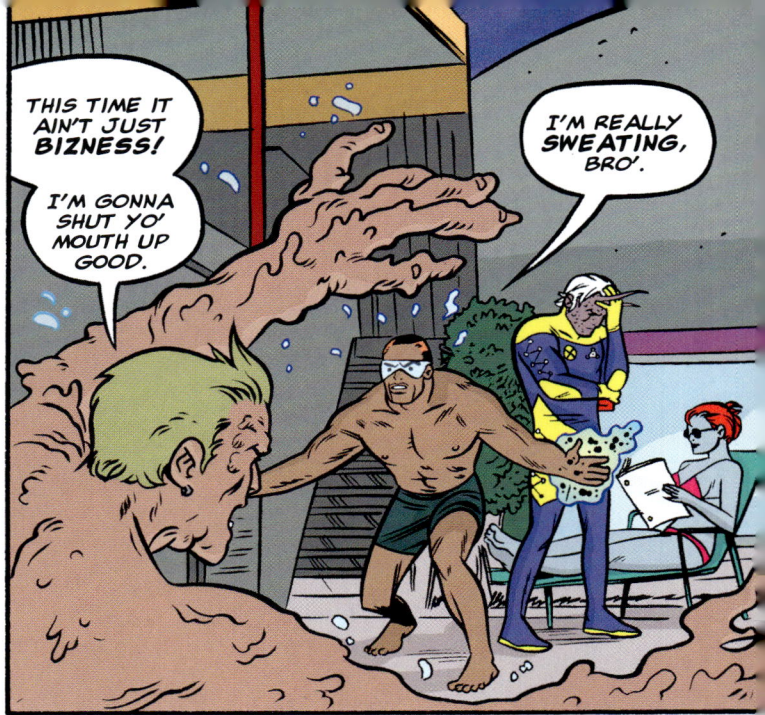

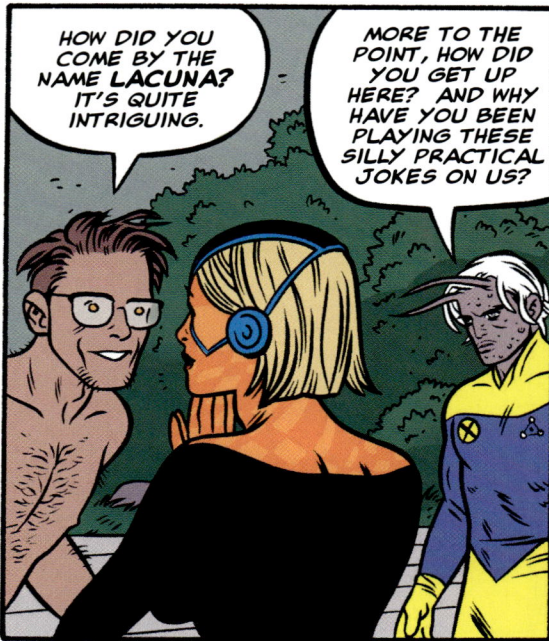

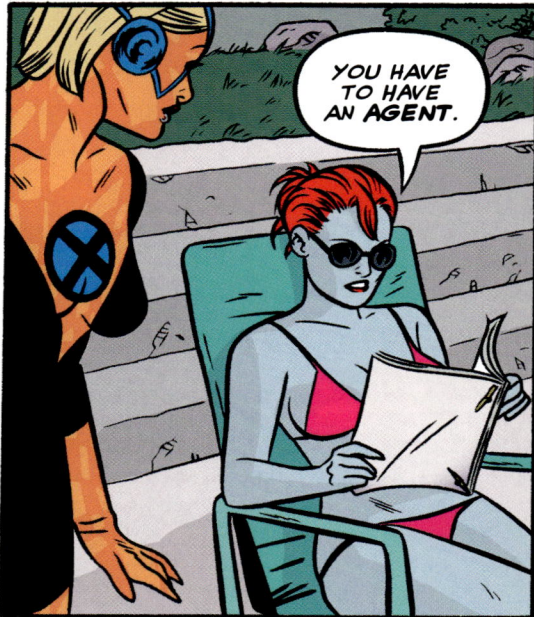

ALL OF WHICH CRAZINESS HAS LED ME TO HERE, DRINKING BOURBON ON A ROOF GARDEN IN L.A.--WITH A BUNCH OF CRAZY MUTANTS CALLED *X-FORCE.*

RICH, FAMOUS AND NOT DESTINED TO LIVE LONG.

DON'T EXPECT *ME* TO MAKE ANY *SENSE* OUT OF IT.

STAN LEE PRESENTS

L A C U N A :

PART TWO: LARRY KING HAS THE FLU

PETER MILLIGAN-WRITER   MICHAEL ALLRED-ARTIST

LAURA ALLRED-COLORIST   DOC ALLRED & BLAMBOT-LETTERING   JOHN MIESEGAES-ASST. EDITOR

AXEL ALONSO-EDITOR   JOE QUESADA-CHIEF   BILL JEMAS-PRESIDENT

THE THINGS I'VE BEEN DOING, WITH THE FISH AND THE HATS, THEY WERE JUST TO SHOW HOW *USEFUL* I COULD BE.

I'M SORRY, LACUNA. IT DOESN'T WORK THAT WAY.

HELL, WHY NOT? SHE GETS MY VOTE. LET HER INTO THE PARTY.

NEW MEMBERS HAVE GOT TO HAVE PROVEN TRACK RECORDS. OTHERWISE IT'LL BE LIKE HANDING DOWN A DEATH SENTENCE.

I'M WILLING TO DIE FOR X-FORCE.

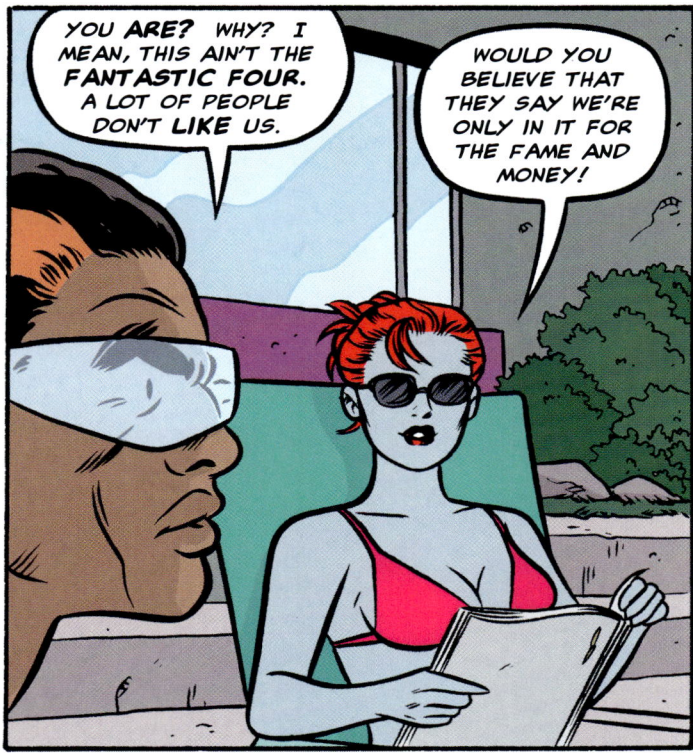

YOU **ARE?** WHY? I MEAN, THIS AIN'T THE **FANTASTIC FOUR.** A LOT OF PEOPLE DON'T **LIKE** US.

WOULD YOU BELIEVE THAT THEY SAY WE'RE ONLY IN IT FOR THE FAME AND MONEY!

THAT'S JUST THE IMAGE YOU PROJECT. BECAUSE YOU REPRESENT THE NEW WORLD. A WORLD WHERE THE OLD TRUTHS HAVE BEEN BLOWN AWAY.

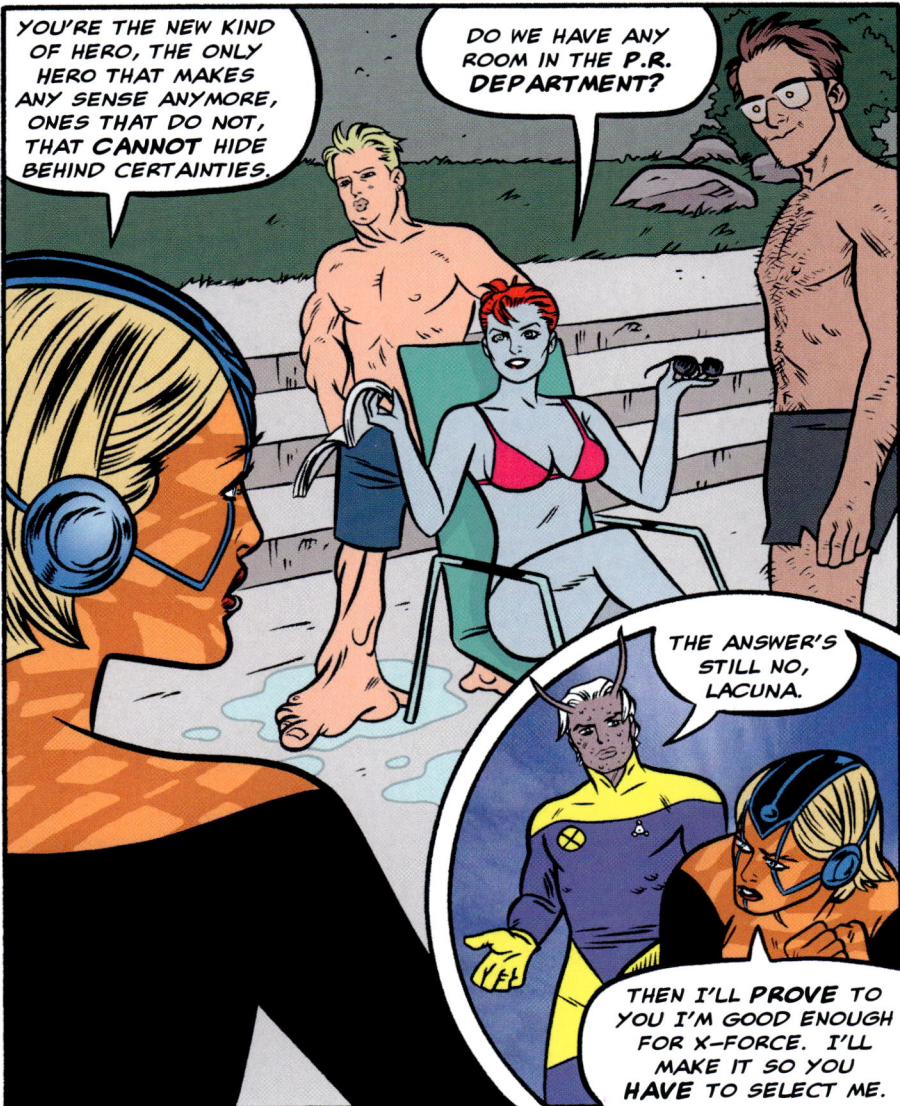

YOU'RE THE NEW KIND OF HERO, THE ONLY HERO THAT MAKES ANY SENSE ANYMORE, ONES THAT DO NOT, THAT **CANNOT** HIDE BEHIND CERTAINTIES.

DO WE HAVE ANY ROOM IN THE P.R. DEPARTMENT?

THE ANSWER'S STILL NO, LACUNA.

THEN I'LL **PROVE** TO YOU I'M GOOD ENOUGH FOR X-FORCE. I'LL MAKE IT SO YOU **HAVE** TO SELECT ME.

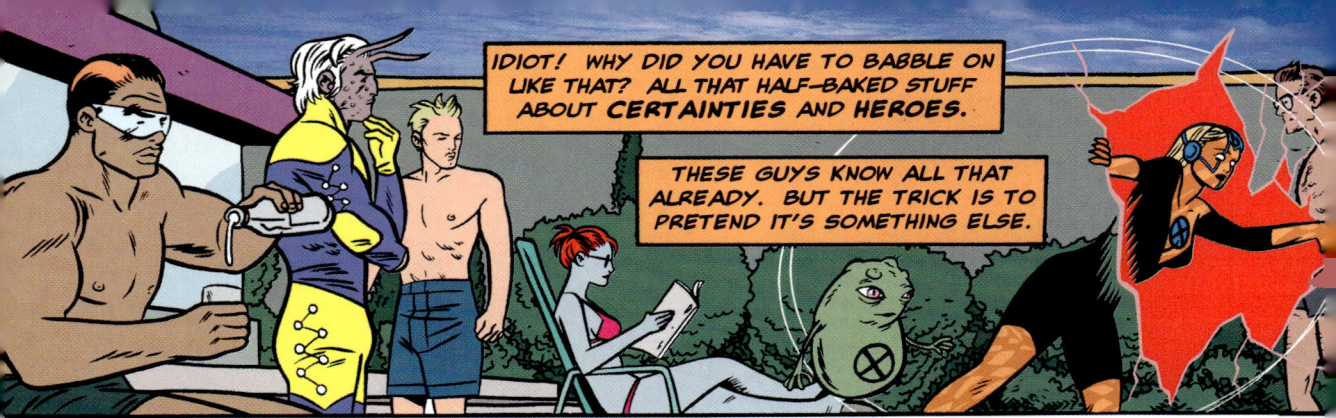

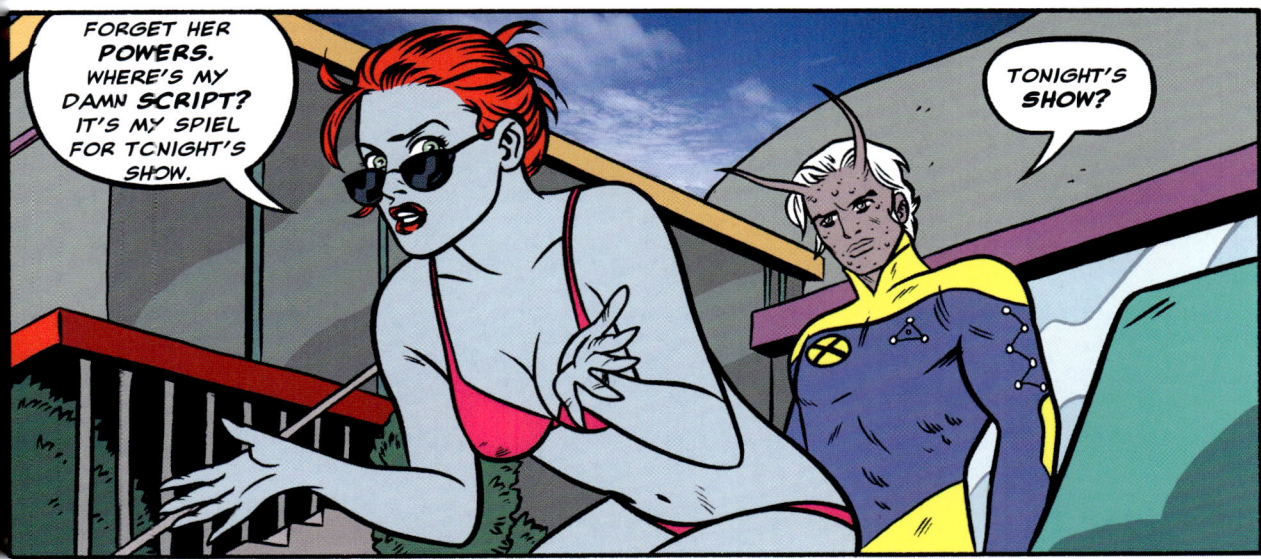

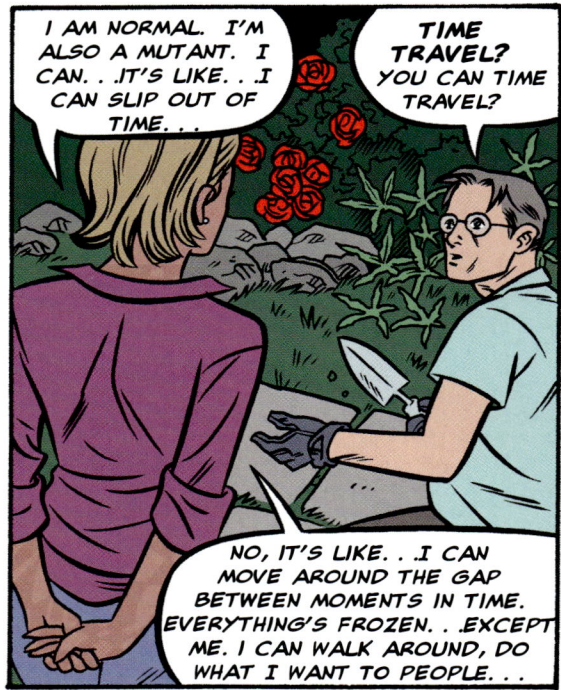

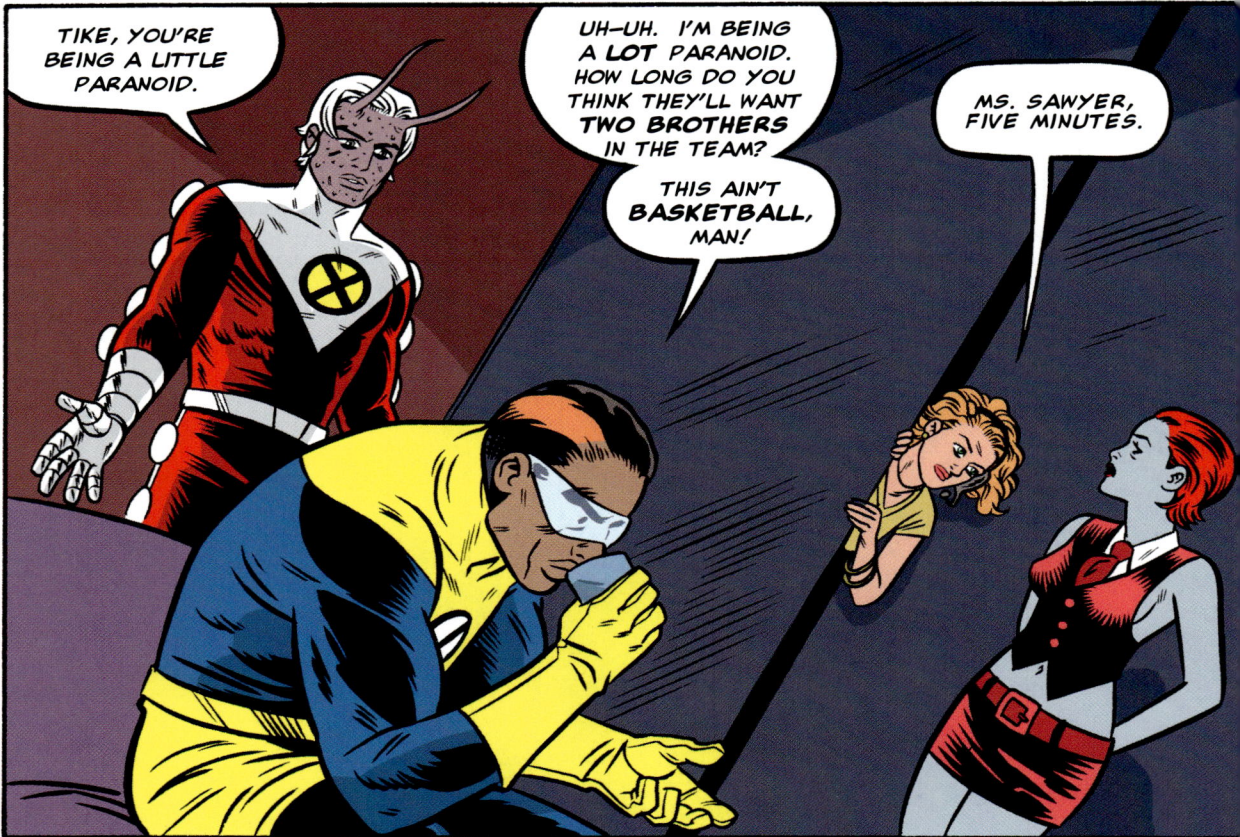

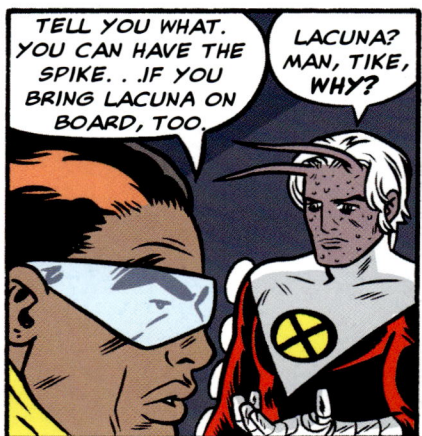

I DON'T NEED ANY HELP, DAD. THIS IS SOMETHING I'VE GOT TO DO ON MY OWN.

MAYBE WE COULD MAKE SOME KIND OF DIVERSION. YOUR FATHER AND I COULD START TO MAKE LOVE...

NO, MOM. PLEASE! I BEG YOU!

TONIGHT ONLY! EDIE SAWY

TICKETS! LINE FORMS HERE.

IT'S JUST THAT WE'RE SO PROUD, WOODSTOCK. I MEAN, NOW THAT YOU'VE EXPLAINED THAT X-FORCE ARE ONLY PRETENDING TO BE PART OF THE SYSTEM... BUT ARE ACTUALLY AGAINST IT, WE REALLY DIG THE IDEA OF YOU JOINING THEM.

IN MANY WAYS, YOU'RE FOLLOWING IN OUR FOOTSTEPS.

WE REALIZED A FEW YEARS AGO THAT YOU DIDN'T HAVE TO BE POOR TO BE... ALTERNATIVE.

THAT BEING MILLIONAIRES AND LIVING IN A MANSION IN MALIBU DIDN'T MEAN WE WEREN'T AGAINST THE WHOLE GLOBAL CAPITALIST THING.

SAY, ISN'T THAT PHAT AND THE VIVISECTOR?

MAN, THEY'RE HIGH AS KITES.

THOUGH THEY'RE PROBABLY JUST PRETENDING TO BE, RIGHT?

AH, RIGHT.

I THINK THIS IS GOING TO BE SOME SHOW.

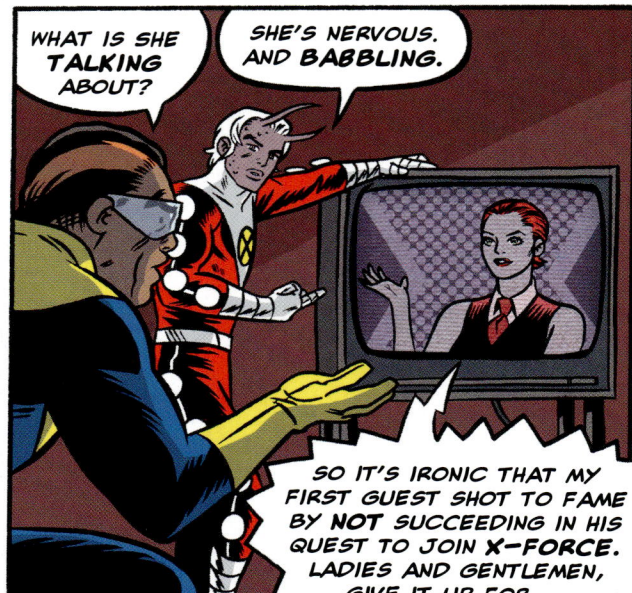

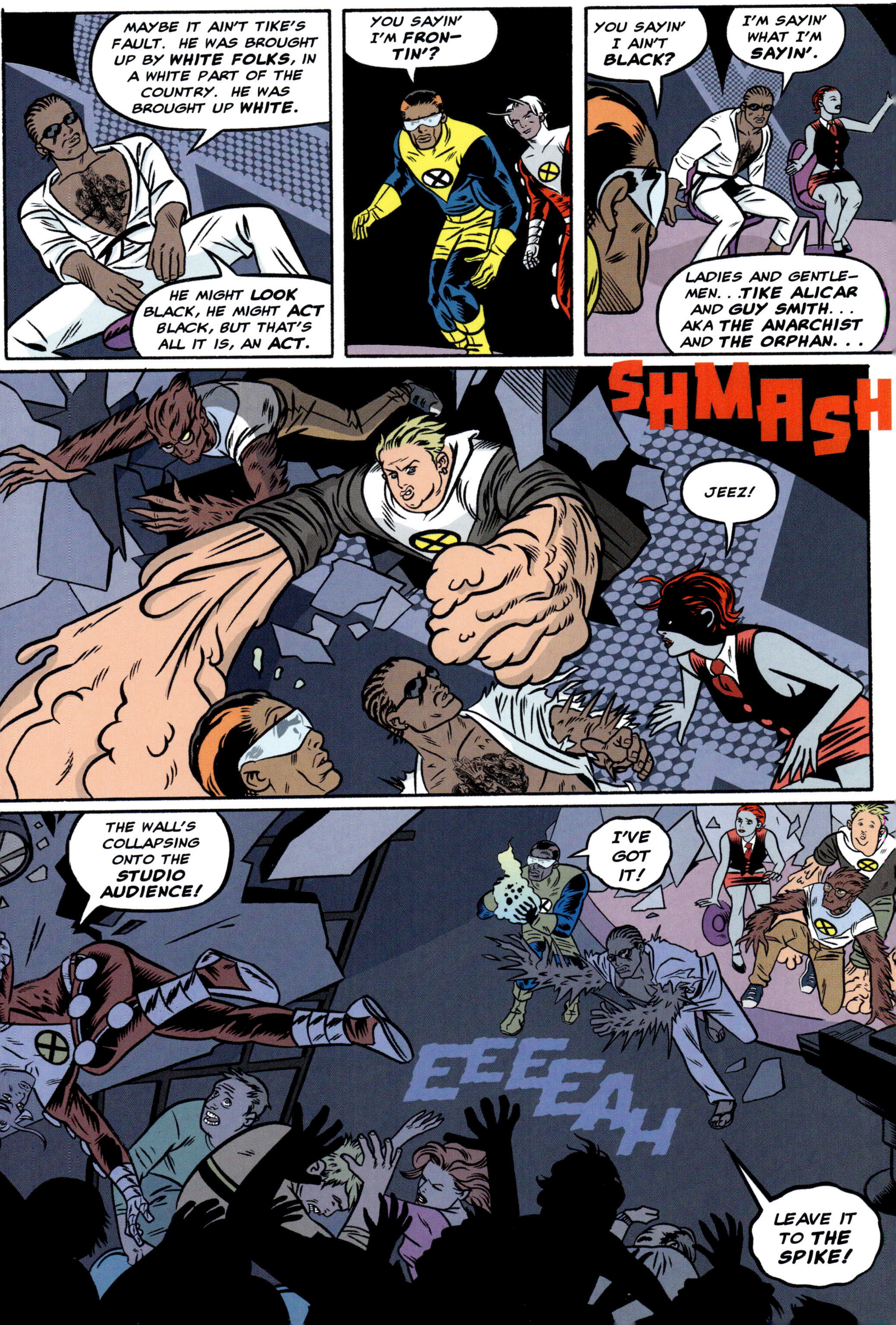
MAYBE IT AIN'T TIKE'S FAULT. HE WAS BROUGHT UP BY WHITE FOLKS, IN A WHITE PART OF THE COUNTRY. HE WAS BROUGHT UP WHITE.
HE MIGHT LOOK BLACK, HE MIGHT ACT BLACK, BUT THAT'S ALL IT IS, AN ACT.
YOU SAYIN' I'M FRON-TIN'?
YOU SAYIN' I AIN'T BLACK?
I'M SAYIN' WHAT I'M SAYIN'.
LADIES AND GENTLE-MEN. . .TIKE ALICAR AND GUY SMITH. . . AKA THE ANARCHIST AND THE ORPHAN. . .
SHMASH
JEEZ!
THE WALL'S COLLAPSING ONTO THE STUDIO AUDIENCE!
I'VE GOT IT!
EEEEAH
LEAVE IT TO THE SPIKE!

I HANG A LITTLE WITH THOSE OTHER TWO NUMBSKULLS. FIGURE IT CAN'T DO ANY HARM TO HEDGE MY BETS.

I HAVE A FEELING THAT GUY AND EDIE WILL BE GETTING IT ON SOON, AND THEN WHO KNOWS HOW THIS DELICATE BALANCE OF POWER WILL SHIFT.

I GUESS IT'S ALL SOMETHING OF A **CRAP-SHOOT.**

YOU'VE WON AGAIN.

NO SWEAT!

BACK HOME, I PACE AROUND FOR A WHILE BEFORE DOING WHAT I **REALLY** WANT TO DO.

THEN SOMETHING STOPS ME. IT'S WEIRD, A WEIRD FEELING. ON MY **LIPS.**

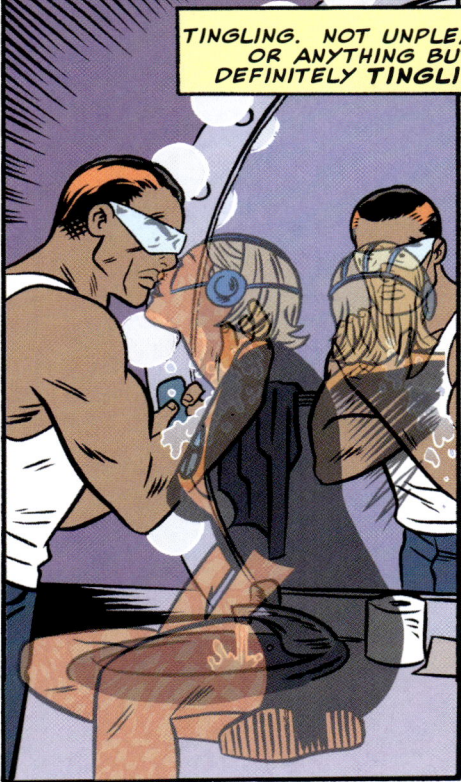

TINGLING. NOT UNPLEASANT OR ANYTHING BUT DEFINITELY **TINGLING.**

COME ON, MY HANDS ARE PROBABLY FILTHY AFTER HANDLING ALL THOSE **DICE** AND ALL THAT **MONEY!**

HELL, FEELS LIKE I'VE JUST BEEN **KISSED.**

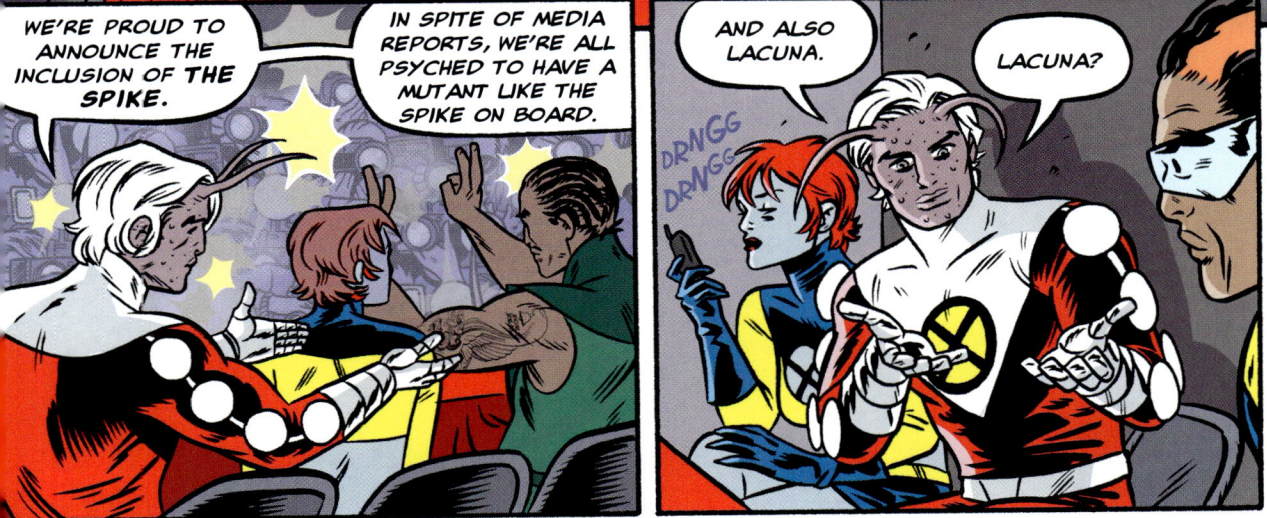

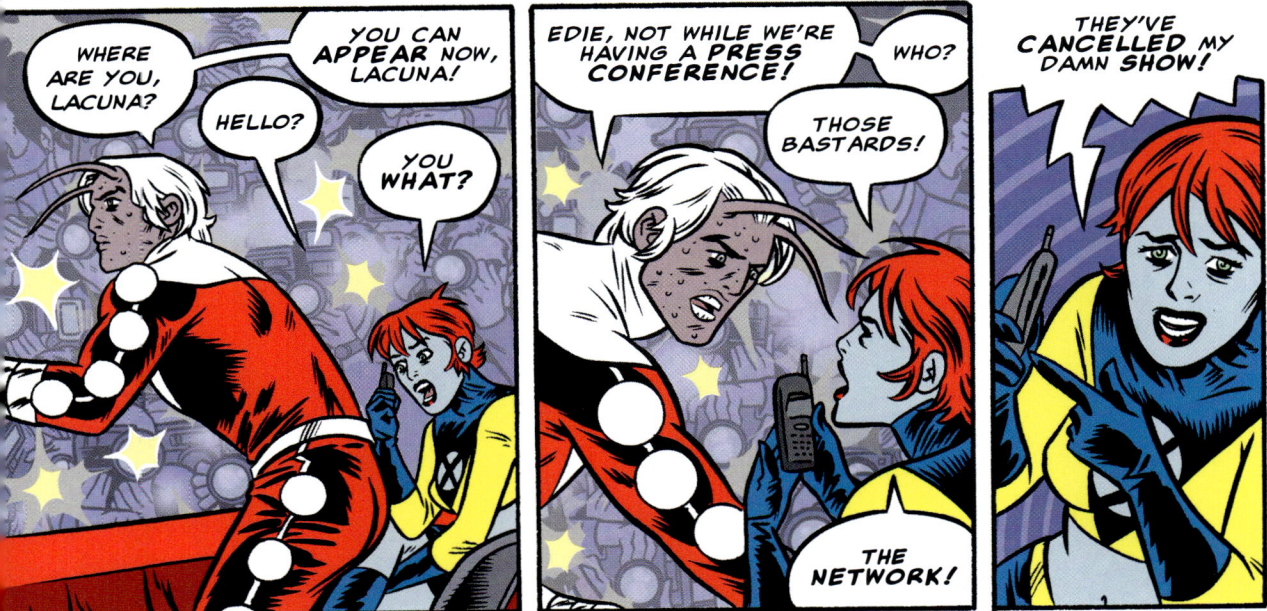

ALL OF WHICH CRAZINESS LEADS HERE.
COME ON, FELLAS. WE'RE GOING TO HAVE TO MAKE A DECISION. I KNOW DEAD GIRL IS A LITTLE WEIRD BUT I THINK SHE HAS REAL POTENTIAL.
THOUGH SHE'S NOT REALLY THE KIND OF GIRL YOU'D WANT TO TAKE HOME TO MOTHER.
THAT VENUS DEE MILO IS A BABE.
NO, I AM NOT WILLING TO ADVERTISE LIFT AND SEPARATE BRAS. AND IF THAT'S THE BEST YOU CAN FIND FOR ME, I MIGHT JUST HAVE TO START TALKING TO WILLIAM MORRIS.
IS IT ME. . .OR IS THIS POPCORN, LIKE, STALE?
POP CORN
BUT DON'T EXPECT ME TO MAKE ANY SENSE OUT OF IT.

TICK

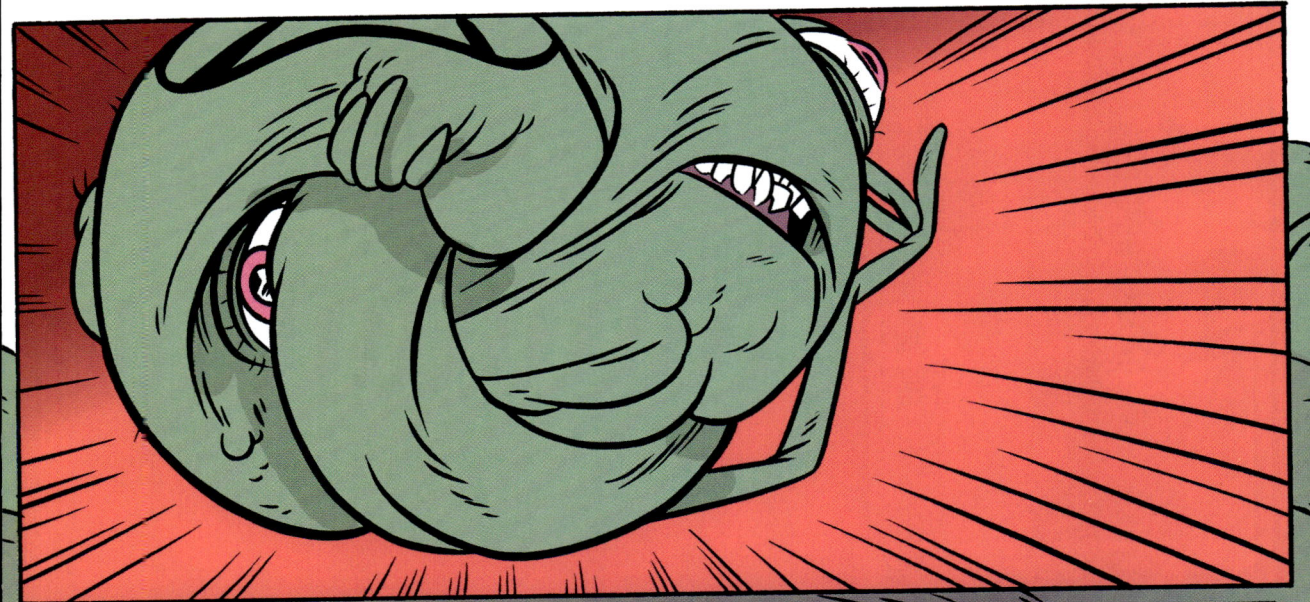

TOCK

OUR WORK HERE IS DONE. TAKE US HOME, EDIE.
WHAT DO YOU THINK I'M DOING? MY AEROBIC EXERCISES?

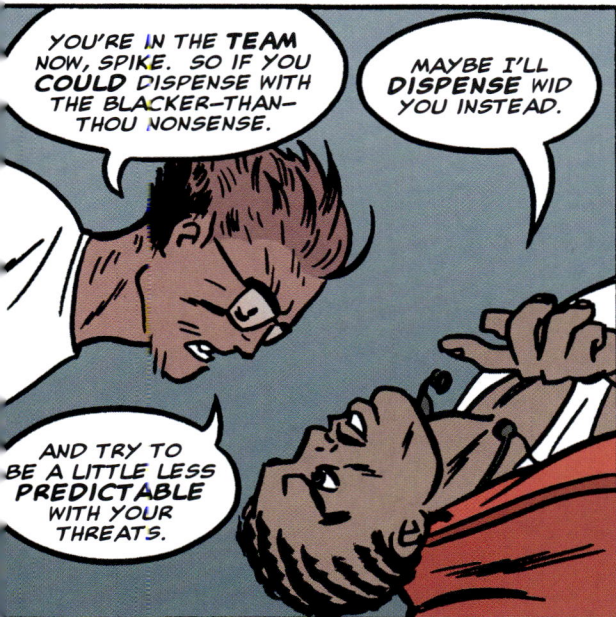

Edie Constance Sawyer.

Listening to the branches of the willow tree tip-tapping on the window.

Wishing I was somewhere-anywhere-else.

I was about twelve when it started. I'd go to sleep in my bed and wake up in the strangest places.

They put it down to sleepwalking.

Ma was worried about it but the doctor said I'd grow out of it. I hoped I didn't.

It was a quiet house. Pa didn't like music. Didn't like TV. He said the noise made it hard for him to think.

But what the hell did he think about?

I'd catch him sometimes looking at me like I was a stranger who'd just walked through the door.

Which is pretty much how I felt.

I BOUGHT A CRAPPY LITTLE TV FROM MCGINLEY'S AND PRACTICED TALKING LIKE THE PEOPLE I WATCHED.

I DIDN'T CARE IF THE ACCENT WAS WEST COAST, NEW ENGLAND OR *BRITISH*, I *WANTED* IT.

I KNOW, JUST YOUR EVERYDAY, RUN-OF-THE-MILL, DISAFFECTED, ALIENATED TEENAGER. BUT YOU THINK YOU'RE THE ONLY PERSON WHO HAS EVER FELT LIKE THAT.

YOU WANTED TO BE LIVING IN A DIFFERENT WORLD. LIVING A DIFFERENT LIFE.

MILLIONS OF THE SELF-PITYING LITTLE PUNKS, ALL THINKING THEY'RE UNIQUE.

AND THEY ARE. EACH ONE OF THEM.

YOUR SLEEPWALKING. THAT WAS OBVIOUSLY AN EARLY SIGN OF YOUR POWER TO *TELEPORT*.

I KNOW THAT NOW.

YOUR SUBCONSCIOUS WAS ACCESSING YOUR LATENT POWER TO GIVE YOU WHAT YOU WANT: TO GET AWAY.

IS THIS *MY* STORY OR *YOURS*?

SORRY.

DO YOU WANT TO GO ON?

YEAH.

LET'S KEEP WALKING.

He was from San Francisco. Seventeen years old, passing through, and he made me laugh.

And we kept walking 'til we got to the stream.

When I couldn't hide it any more, I thought they'd kick me out. Maybe I wanted them to. But Ma just held me and cried.

I'd never heard my parents argue before. Can't really remember them talking to each other at all.

SHE'S FIFTEEN YEARS OLD.

EXACTLY.

I'M NOT GOING TO LOSE MY DAUGHTER.

YOUR DAUGHTER.

OUR DAUGHTER.

YOU WERE RIGHT THE FIRST TIME.

WHY DO YOU WANT ME TO FEEL GUILTY... ABOUT SOMETHING WE BOTH AGREED ON? SOMETHING WE BOTH WANTED?

Turns out Pa wasn't really my Pa. He couldn't have kids so he and Ma had come to some kind of arrangement.

My real father was some guy passing through town. Must run in the family.

I was pulled out of school. Kept hidden from everyone.

And Ma made out she was pregnant again. Even went to church with a pillow stuffed under her dress.

And then the day came. I wasn't scared or excited or anything. It was like it was happening to another person.

I heard its first scream. Amazing how something so small could make such a racket.

IT'S A GIRL!

TAKE A LOOK AT YOUR LITTLE BABY GIRL, EDIE.

And so I looked into that little red scrunched up, impossibly beautiful little face.

And had to get away.

This one was a little harder to blame on sleepwalking.

The next time I went home, the next time I saw... my daughter... was with you guys.

HOLLYW

EDIE. . . YOU ASLEEP?
NOT EVEN CLOSE.
MOT
THESE WALLS ARE REAL THIN.
I KNOW. I CAN HEAR YOU BREATHING.
YOU CAN?
AND I CAN FEEL THE BEAT OF YOUR HEART VIBRATING DOWN THE WALL. IT'S A LITTLE FAST. WHAT ARE YOU FRETTING ABOUT?
I DON'T WANT TO GO HOME TOMORROW. I DON'T WANT TO SEE THEM ALL AGAIN. I'VE TOLD YOU EVERYTHING THERE IS TO KNOW.
TOO BAD. WE'RE GOING.
YOU CAN BE SO ANNOYING.
I KNOW.

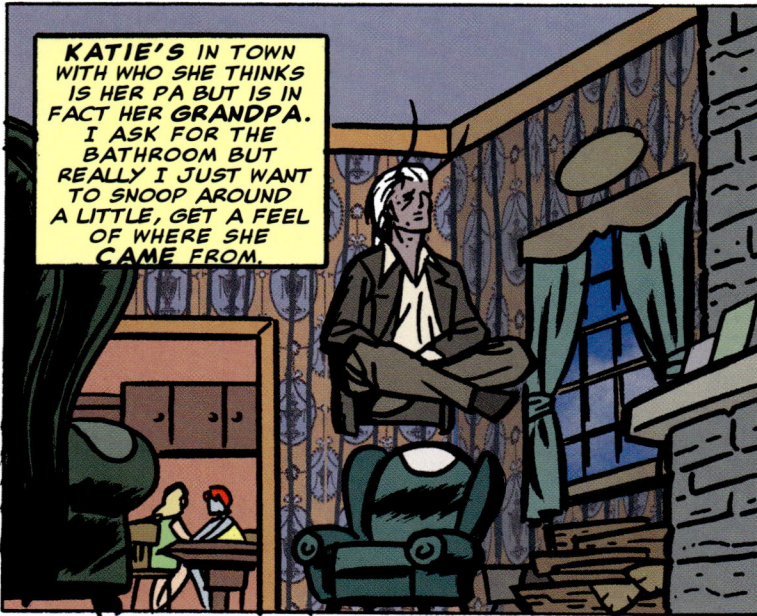

WELL... AIN'T YOU GOT A **HUG** FOR YOUR...

...**BIG SISTER?**

SO THEY LAUGH AND CRY SOME MORE. EXCEPT EDIE'S **PA**, WHO NODS TO EDIE AS THOUGH SHE'D JUST COME BACK FROM BUYING **GROCERIES.**

KATIE... KATIE WANTS ME TO TAKE HER 'PORTING...

I DON'T WANT TO DISAPPOINT HER BUT... JEEZ, GUY... I'M NOT SURE IF I'M **UP** TO IT.

WHAT THE HELL ARE YOU TALKING ABOUT? YOU'RE **EDIE SAWYER!** YOU'RE **U-GO GIRL!** OF COURSE YOU'RE DAMN WELL **UP** TO IT!

I HIT EVERY TARGET DEAD CENTER. NO WOBBLES. NO ENDING UP DROWNING IN ICE COLD WATER.
AND NOW YOU'RE GOING TO TELL ME WHY I WAS ABLE TO 'PORT AGAIN.
TRY TO STOP ME.
YOUR 'PORTING BEGAN AS AN UNCONSCIOUS ATTEMPT TO FLEE FROM YOUR OLD LIFE, AND YOUR OLD SELF.
BUT THEN YOU REACHED A STAGE IN YOUR LIFE WHEN YOU DIDN'T NEED TO RUN FROM THE PAST ANYMORE. AND SO INDIRECTLY YOU'RE 'PORTING BACK TO YOUR OLD HOME. . .
THAT'S WHAT YOU THINK, SMARTY PANTS.
TRUTH IS, I PICKED UP SOME SUPER NEW CONCOCTION FROM SPIKE FREEMAN BEFORE WE LEFT. . . DOES WONDERS FOR MY CONCENTRATION! SORRY TO SPOIL YOUR POP PSYCHOLOGY CLASS.
HOWEVER YOU GOT YOUR OLD MAGIC BACK. . . COULD YOU MANAGE ONE MORE 'PORT? THIS ROAD IS GOING ON FOREVER.
WHAT DID YOU HAVE IN MIND?

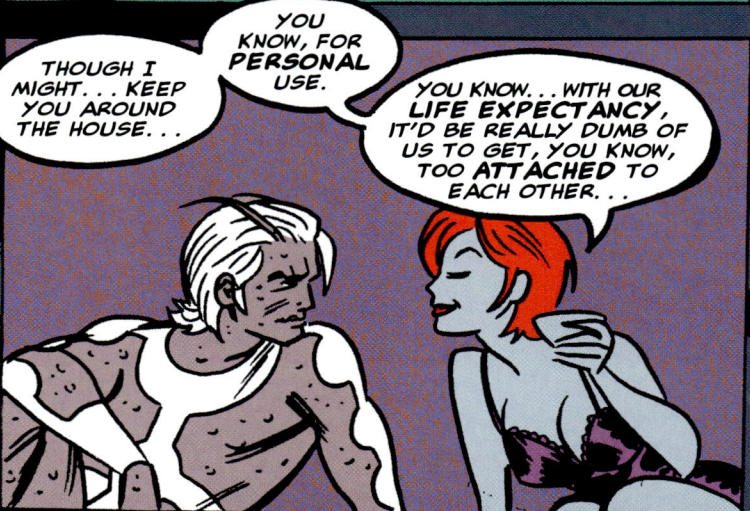

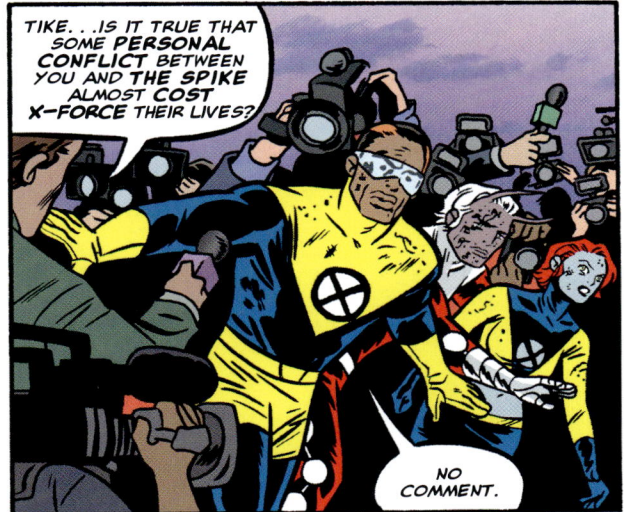

EDIE WAS RIGHT. IT WAS NASTY AND MESSY...

...THOUGH IT WAS SUPPOSED TO BE NICE AND SIMPLE.

A SURGICAL STRIKE INTO A CENTRAL AMERICAN STATE TO FIND AND ARREST A GENERAL WANTED FOR CRIMES AGAINST HUMANITY.

JUST THE KIND OF MISSION TO COUNTER OUR REP AS CHAMPAGNE-MUTANTS.

IT GOT VERY BAD.

THE RIVALRY BETWEEN TIKE AND SPIKE GOT DANGEROUSLY INSANE.

I DON'T THINK EITHER WERE AWARE OF ANYTHING BUT EACH OTHER.

MYLES AND PHAT SEEMED INCREASINGLY ISOLATED. LIKE A TEAM WITHIN A TEAM. SOMETHING WEIRD GOING ON.

AND THEN THERE WERE EDIE AND ME.

I TRIED TO BE PROFESSIONAL BUT FOUND MYSELF GIVING HER AN ORDER PURELY TO GET HER OUT OF THE FIRING LINE.

IF YOU EVER DO THAT AGAIN WE'RE FINISHED, UNDERSTAND?

FINISHED.

I'M SORRY, EDIE, BUT...

THEN WE HAD TO STALL MOVING IN ON THE GENERAL SO THE NETWORKS COULD BE THERE TO FILM IT, TO MAKE IT REAL.

NO X-FORCE

NO X-FORCE

X-FORCE

REVOLUCION SI NO MUTANT

ABA EL 'CR BARR

MUERA LOS T ...PEN NO

GO HO X-FO

YANKIS GO HOME

DURING WHICH TIME WE LEARNED THAT OUR PRESENCE WASN'T AS UNANIMOUSLY WELCOMED AS WE'D BEEN LED TO BELIEVE.

FOR THE RECORD, THE CIVILIAN DEATH COUNT WAS BETWEEN *SIX* AND *EIGHTEEN*, DEPENDING ON YOUR *POLITICS*.

MAYBE A CHANGE OF *NAME* WILL HELP RESTORE YOUR IMAGE.

YOU THINK IT'S THAT SIMPLE?

I'M GOING TO BED.

OKAY... I MUST ADMIT I HAVE MY OWN REASONS FOR WANTING A CHANGE OF NAME.

YOU'RE AN ANALLY-RETENTIVE OVER-GROWN SCHOOLBOY WITH TOO MUCH MONEY?

WE DON'T ACTUALLY *OWN* THE NAME *X-FORCE*.

WE *DON'T?*

IT'S A LEGAL THING. BUT SOME OF THE ORIGINAL FOUNDERS STILL HAVE A PIECE OF IT...WHICH MEANS I HAVE TO SEND THEM AN IRRITATING CHECK EVERY MONTH.

COME ON, YOU'RE A NEW TEAM. COME UP WITH A NEW NAME! AS LONG AS IT'S GOT THAT *X* IN IT.

BY THE WAY... HAVE YOU DECIDED ON YOUR *NEW RECRUIT* YET?

MARKETING CAN ALWAYS USE *FRESH BLOOD*.

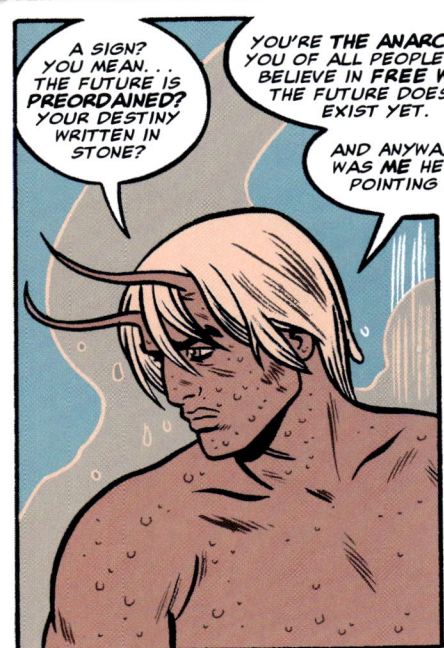

GETTING LESS SURE BY THE MINUTE.

JEEZ, GUY, ARE YOU ALL RIGHT?

YEAH. I COULDN'T HELP IT. SOMETHING... SOMETHING JUST SNAPPED.

SURE AS HELL SOMETHING SNAPPED. HIS LILY-LIVERED, BLEEDING-HEART MUTANT BACK-BONE IS WHAT SNAPPED.

HE AIN'T A MAN. HE'S A JELLY-FISH.

JELLYFISH DON'T HAVE BACKBONES.

YOU SHOULD BE MORE CAREFUL WHO YOU'RE MIXING IT WITH.

I...I WAS MIXING A METAPHOR.

EDIE... LEAVE IT!

HOW ABOUT... THE X-FOLIATES?

BRO, AIN'T THAT A LITTLE TOO GAY?

PHAT, CAN ANYTHING BE TOO GAY?

LISTEN GOOD, C.I.A AGENT WRIGHT. YOU MIGHT THINK WE'RE A BUNCH OF TINSEL-TOWN LIGHTWEIGHTS THAT YOU CAN PUSH AROUND...
BUT IF YOU DO ANYTHING TO HARM GUY SMITH YOU WILL HAVE ME TO CONTEND WITH.
PLEASE, DEAR GOD, PLEASE, WE'RE FALLING!

IT SEEMS SOME REAL POWERFUL MULTINATIONAL PHARMACEUTICAL COMPANIES ARE... UPSET THAT YOU DIDN'T HAND LITTLE **PACO PEREZ** OVER TO THEM.

WE HAD NO **CHOICE!** THEY WERE GOING TO MURDER HIM. TREAT HIM LIKE HE WAS... A **COMMODITY**, TO BE STRIPPED OF ITS ASSETS.

I **KNOW** THAT...

BUT NOW IT'S **OUR** ASSETS THAT ARE ON THE LINE, RIGHT?

RIGHT. THOSE MULTINATIONALS WANT BLOOD. **YOUR** BLOOD, GUY. THEY WANT TO DESTROY YOU. AND BY EXTENSION, **X-FORCE.**

COME ON, **EDIE!** HOW THEY GONNA DO **THAT?**

FOR **STARTERS**, THEY'RE GOING TO BEAM WORLDWIDE COMMERCIALS FEATURING **KIDS** WITH **TERMINAL ILLNESSES**, EXPLAINING HOW THEY'D HAVE A CHANCE TO LIVE IF IT WEREN'T FOR **YOU.**

I SEE.

RIGHT.

I GUESS THAT WOULD DO IT.

THERE WAS A MOMENT. NO.

THERE WAS AN **OPPORTUNITY**.

I DON'T KNOW WHAT IT **WAS**.

BUT THERE WERE DEAD ADULTS, AND THERE WAS A YOUNG CHILD. A GIRL, I THINK.

THIS WAS BACK IN LATIN AMERICA, THE CLEAN SURGICAL STRIKE, YOU REMEMBER...

THE ROOM STUNK OF URINE AND FECES AND...**ONIONS**.

AND I LOOKED AT HER. I COULD HAVE PICKED HER UP. CARRIED HER AWAY. I HAD THE **POWER**.

LIFE OR DEATH FOR ALL I KNOW.

AND I WALKED AWAY.

I GOT ON WITH MY MISSION AND MY LIFE JUST LIKE EVERY OTHER SCARED AND CONFUSED SOUL WHO WALKS AWAY FROM THESE MOMENTS.

IS THAT WHY **DEATH**, THE **GRIM REAPER**, WHATEVER YOU WANNA CALL IT...

...IS THAT WHY HE POINTED AT **ME**?

UH, MR. SMITH, ARE YOU LISTENING, MR. SMITH? THIS IS IMPORTANT.

AH. . .SORRY. . . MIND WAS ELSEWHERE.

CARRY ON.

FOR SOME REASON, THE *C.I.A. AGENT* IS TREATING ME WITH A LOT MORE *RESPECT.*

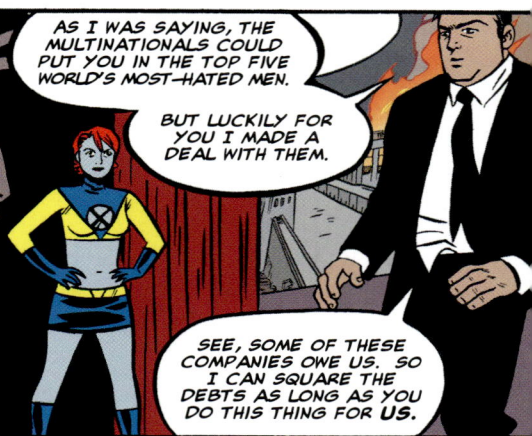

AS I WAS SAYING, THE MULTINATIONALS COULD PUT YOU IN THE TOP FIVE WORLD'S MOST-HATED MEN.

BUT LUCKILY FOR YOU I MADE A DEAL WITH THEM.

SEE, SOME OF THESE COMPANIES OWE US. SO I CAN SQUARE THE DEBTS AS LONG AS YOU DO THIS THING FOR *US.*

REMEMBER LAST YEAR, THERE WAS A FIRE AT THE *TEXAS STATE PENITENTIARY.* RAGED THROUGH THE DEATH ROW CELLS KILLING EIGHTEEN CONDEMNED INMATES.

MATT BUCHANAN SAID IT WAS THE FIRE OF GOD'S RETRIBUTION.

FACT IS, IT WASN'T GOD, IT WAS THE C.I.A.

WHO SIMPLY LIKE *PLAYING* GOD.

AND THE INMATES DIDN'T DIE IN THE FIRE.

THEY'D ALL AGREED TO SIGN UP FOR A SECRET AND EXPERIMENTAL PROCEDURE.

THE IDEA WAS TO MANUFACTURE OUR *OWN MUTANTS,* WHOM WE COULD *CONTROL.*

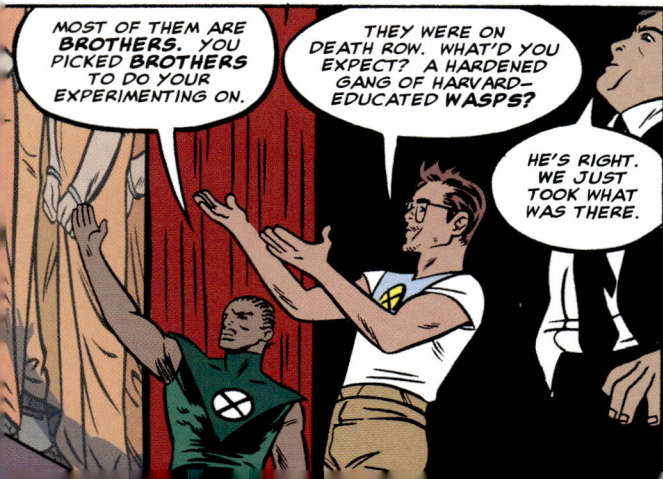

MOST OF THEM ARE *BROTHERS.* YOU PICKED *BROTHERS* TO DO YOUR EXPERIMENTING ON.

THEY WERE ON DEATH ROW. WHAT'D YOU EXPECT? A HARDENED GANG OF HARVARD-EDUCATED *WASPS?*

HE'S RIGHT. WE JUST TOOK WHAT WAS THERE.

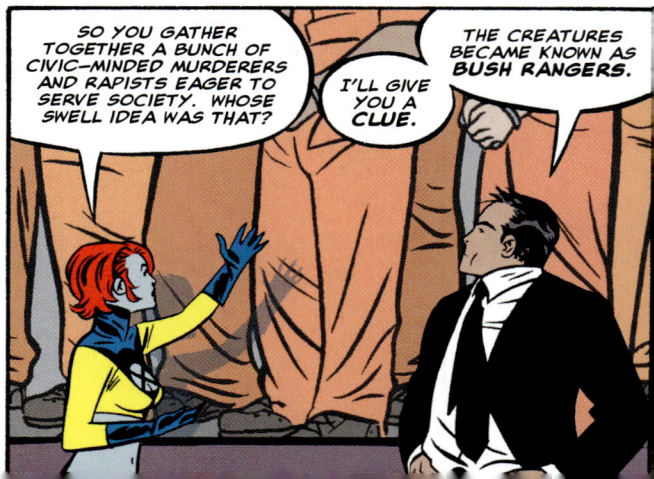

SO YOU GATHER TOGETHER A BUNCH OF CIVIC-MINDED MURDERERS AND RAPISTS EAGER TO SERVE SOCIETY. WHOSE SWELL IDEA WAS THAT?

I'LL GIVE YOU A *CLUE.*

THE CREATURES BECAME KNOWN AS *BUSH RANGERS.*

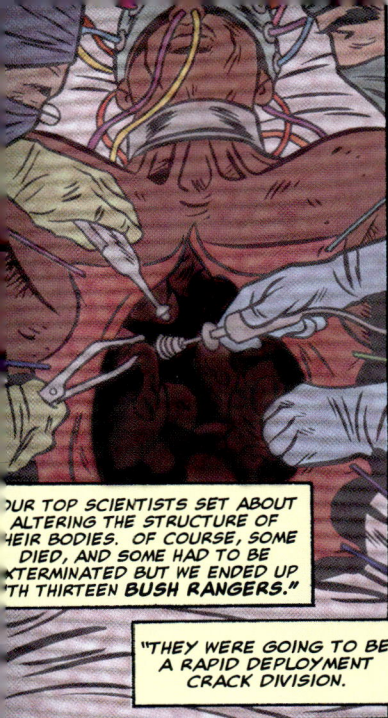

"OUR TOP SCIENTISTS SET ABOUT ALTERING THE STRUCTURE OF THEIR BODIES. OF COURSE, SOME DIED, AND SOME HAD TO BE EXTERMINATED BUT WE ENDED UP WITH THIRTEEN **BUSH RANGERS**."

"THEY WERE GOING TO BE A RAPID DEPLOYMENT CRACK DIVISION.

"PROBLEM IS, THE MUTATIONS ON THEIR BODIES WERE MORE SUCCESSFUL THAN THE WORK ON THEIR **BRAINS** TO TURN THEM INTO COMPLIANT, OBEDIENT SOLDIERS.

"THEY'VE TAKEN OVER THE MARS 2010 SPACE STATION, WHERE THEY WERE BEING TRAINED."

SO FAR WE'VE MANAGED TO KEEP A **NEWS** BLACKOUT.

BUT THE SPIN WE'RE GOING TO PUT ON IT IS THAT THEY'RE **ALIENS**. LESS EMBARRASSING FOR EVERYONE.

SO WHERE DO X-FORCE COME IN?

YOU GO UP THERE TO FIGHT THE, UH, **ALIENS**. YOU FREE THE HOSTAGES. THEN YOU GET INTO TROUBLE. YOU LET THE MONSTERS TAKE **YOU** AS HOSTAGES.

AND **THE AGENCY** RIDES IN ON OUR WHITE CHARGERS. WE SAVE THE DAY. OUR TARNISHED REPUTATION IS RESTORED.

THIS STINKS. IT'S GONNA BE LIKE THE **BOYS R US MASSACRE** ALL OVER.

YOU AIN'T GETTING ME ANYWHERE NEAR THAT FLIPPED-OUT SPACE STATION.

YOU HEARD THE MAN. IF WE DON'T DO THIS, THE **MULTINATIONALS** ARE GONNA HANG US OUT TO DRY!

UH-UH. WHAT THE MAN **SAID** WAS...

...THEY'D HANG **GUY** OUT TO DRY.

IT WAS GUY WHO LET **PACO PEREZ** GO. IT WAS GUY WHO DECIDED ONE KID'S LIFE WAS MORE IMPORTANT THAN ANY DRUGS OR CURES OR WHATEVER THEY MIGHT HAVE GOT FROM HIM.

TIKE IS ABSOLUTELY RIGHT. GUY MADE A UNILATERAL DECISION NOT TO HAND PACO OVER. I DON'T RECALL BEING **CONSULTED** ON THE MATTER.

THE ORPHAN MADE THE CALL. LET HIM TAKE THE **FALL**.

EDIE, I JUST WANT TO SAY... THAT WHAT YOU DID...TURNING DOWN THE CHANCE TO BE LEADER. IT WAS... I MEAN...THANKS. IT WAS... SPECIAL OF YOU.

SPECIAL SCHMECIAL. I LOVE YOU, BUT THAT DOESN'T MEAN I DON'T AIM TO BE LEADER ONE DAY.

BUT I'M NOT SO STUPID AS TO TAKE OVER ON THE VERY MISSION THAT WE ARE GOING TO DELIBERATELY SCREW UP.

COME ON, BABY. OUR SPACESHIP'S WAITING.

SO, THIS IS WHAT X-FORCE IS ALL ABOUT.

GOING OFF TO SAVE THE WORLD FROM ALIENS WHO AREN'T ALIENS. AND KNOWING WE'RE GOING TO LOSE.

AND WONDERING WHICH ONE OF US HAS BEEN POINTED AT BY DEATH.

ONE OF US.

TIKE ALICAR.

EDIE SAWYER.

OR ME.

GUY SMITH.

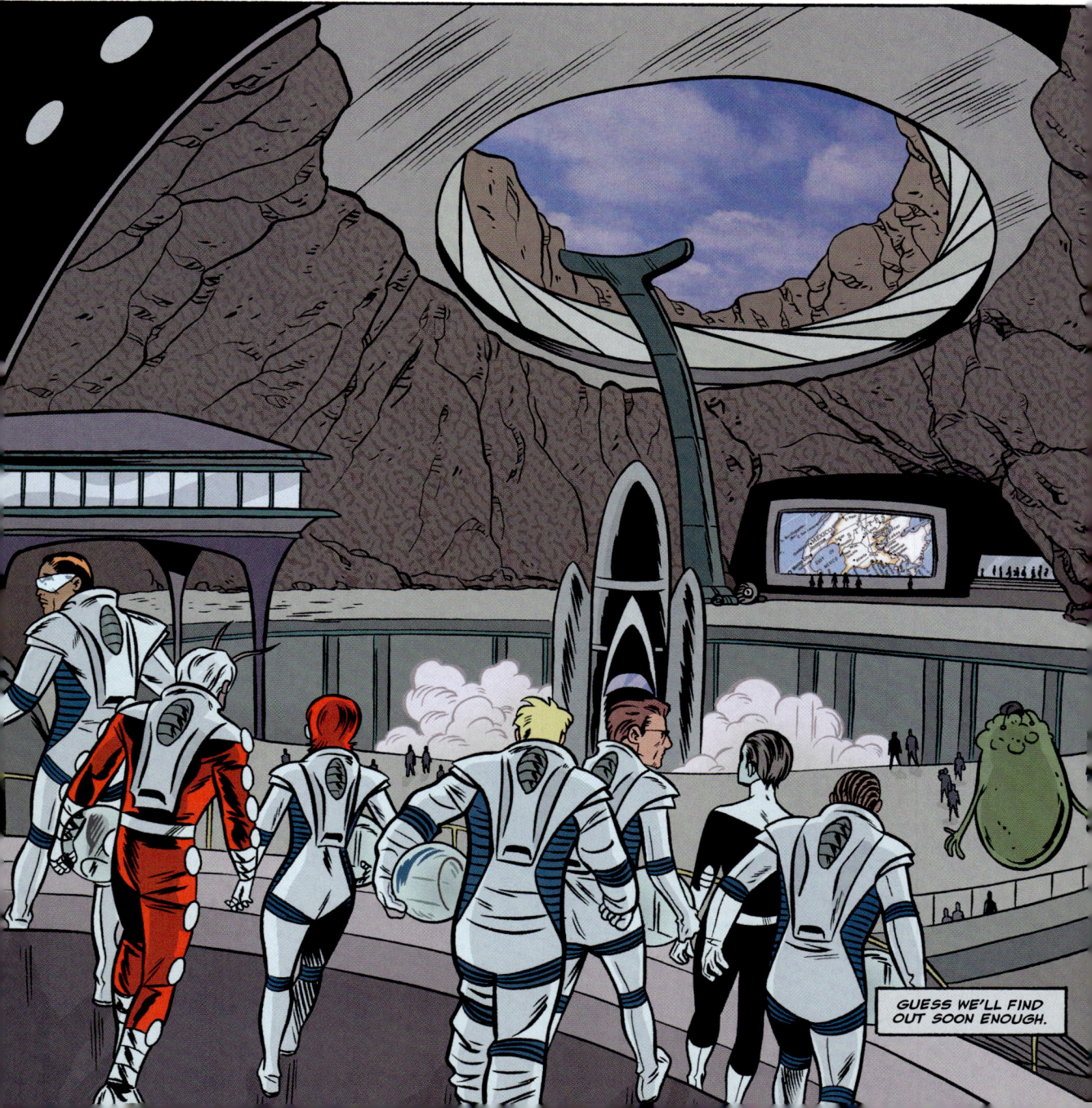

GUESS WE'LL FIND OUT SOON ENOUGH.

WORD IS, SOME HIGH-ROLLERS FROM **MALAYSIA** ARE THROWING SERIOUS DOUGH ON YOU BEING **X-SQUAD.**

FIRST WE'LL SAVE THE PLANET. **THEN** WE'LL WORRY ABOUT WHAT WE'RE CALLED.

IF YOU DON'T KNOW **YOURSELF,** MAYBE YOU'VE GOT SOME **BUDDIES** WHO CAN TELL US.

AND THEN, MAYBE YOU CAN, LIKE, HAVE A **WORD** WITH THEM... TELL THEM THAT ALL THREE OF US ARE NEEDED **ALIVE.**

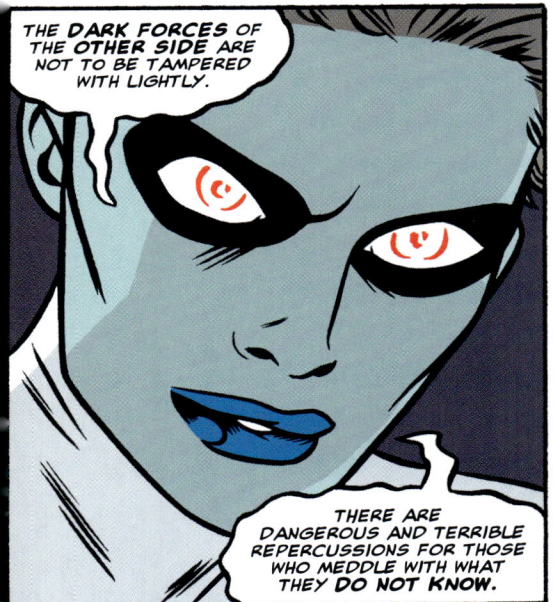

THE **DARK FORCES** OF THE **OTHER SIDE** ARE NOT TO BE TAMPERED WITH LIGHTLY.

THERE ARE DANGEROUS AND TERRIBLE REPERCUSSIONS FOR THOSE WHO MEDDLE WITH WHAT THEY **DO NOT KNOW.**

AND THEN I GIVE THEM MY DELUXE **DEAD GIRL STARE,** A HINT OF FAT MOON SWEATING ON PALE STONE, BLACKENED LEAVES ON BLEACHED BONES, A LOW NOTE OF DECAY.

NOWADAYS, I CAN DO IT WITHOUT **LAUGHING.**

SO... YOU CAN... MAKE **CONTACT?**

I'M CALLED DEAD GIRL, AREN'T I, TIKE ALICAR?

THERE'S SOMEONE OVER THERE I'D LIKE TO... UH... SPEAK TO... OR AT LEAST... MAKE SURE HE'S ALL **RIGHT.**

HE'S NAMED... **ZEITGEIST...** I MEAN... AXEL.

AXEL CLUNEY.

I REMEMBER WHEN I WASN'T DEAD. WHEN I WAS WARM. WHEN I BLED, ATE, BREATHED, LIVED.

LOVED.

I REMEMBER.

COMING TO NEW YORK. ALIVE. ALIVE IN THE ALIVEST CITY IN THE WORLD.

I WANTED TO ACT. I NEEDED TO ACT.

I WANTED A STAGE, NOT A CAMERA.

HOW DID IT HAPPEN, THE END?

YES. THAT'S IT. I REMEMBER.

A BOY. A MAN. AN ACTOR. A LIAR. A KILLER.

A SMALL ROOM IN A SMALL HOTEL IN A BIG CITY.

A KISS. ANOTHER. HIS HANDS. MY SKIN. ALIVE.

HIS HANDS.

I DON'T WANT TO REMEMBER.

I DON'T WANT TO REMEMBER THE DARK. WAKING UP IN THE DARK. THE DARK DAMP SMELL.

THE SOUND OF THE WORMS AND THE FIDGETING OF THE LIVING CITY ALL AROUND.

SOMEHOW, I REMEMBERED WHAT HAD HAPPENED.

HE MUST HAVE THOUGHT HE WAS SO CLEVER.

IT WAS SO CLEVER, BURYING A BODY HERE.

WHO WOULD LOOK FOR A MISSING PERSON HERE, AMONG THE DEAD?

BUT LIFE TEEMS THROUGH THE FORGOTTEN SINEWS OF THE DEAD.

THE DEAD, THE REAL DEAD, THEY TOOK PITY ON ME, MY LONG WEEKS OF WAILING,

OR MAYBE THEY JUST GOT PISSED HAVING SUCH A NOISY NEIGHBOR.

FOR WHATEVER REASON, THE DEAD, THE REAL DEAD, THEY FOUND MY KILLER. IN HIS SMALL ROOM. REHEARSING LINES.

THEY WHISPERED NEW LINES INTO HIS LIVING EAR.

IS SHE DEAD? IS SHE FOUND? IS SHE DISCOVERED? SHOULDN'T YOU BE SURE?

HE HAD TO BE SURE.

I REMEMBER, LYING IN THE DARKNESS.

AND THEN NOISES ABOVE ME.

THE FIRST CRACK OF LIGHT.

AIEEEEE

THAT'S MY **DAMN TEETH** GRINDING.

WAIT! HOLD UP! WE DIDN'T WANNA HURT YOU.

THEN WHAT WAS THAT SHOT IN THE BACK? A **BROTHERLY HANDSHAKE**?

THAT WAS BEFORE WE SAW WHO YOU **WERE**. WE SHOULDN'T BE **FIGHTING** EACH OTHER.

WE'RE ON THE **SAME SIDE**, MAN.

HE'S RIGHT. WE DIDN'T WANNA BE TURNED INTO MUTANTS. BUT IF WE DIDN'T GET WID THE **PROGRAM** WE WERE GONNA GET THE **LETHAL INJECTION** DOUBLE QUICK.

THAT AIN'T OUR PROBLEM. WE'RE X-FORCE.

YOU'RE **BLACK**.

COME ON, MAN. WE SAW YOU TWO GUYS ON THAT SHOW. . . WHEN YOU CALLED THE ANARCHIST HERE CAPTAIN COCONUT.

BLACK OUTSIDE. WHITE INSIDE.

SO HOW BLACK **ARE** YOU, MAN? WHO YOU REALLY **LOYAL** TO?

DON'T LISTEN, SPIKEY! THEY WERE ON DEATH ROW. THEY'RE **KILLERS**!

WE WERE TRIED AND CONVICTED BY A WHITE RACIST SYSTEM, MAN. YOU KNOW IT'S TRUE!

THEY'RE. . . **RIGHT**.

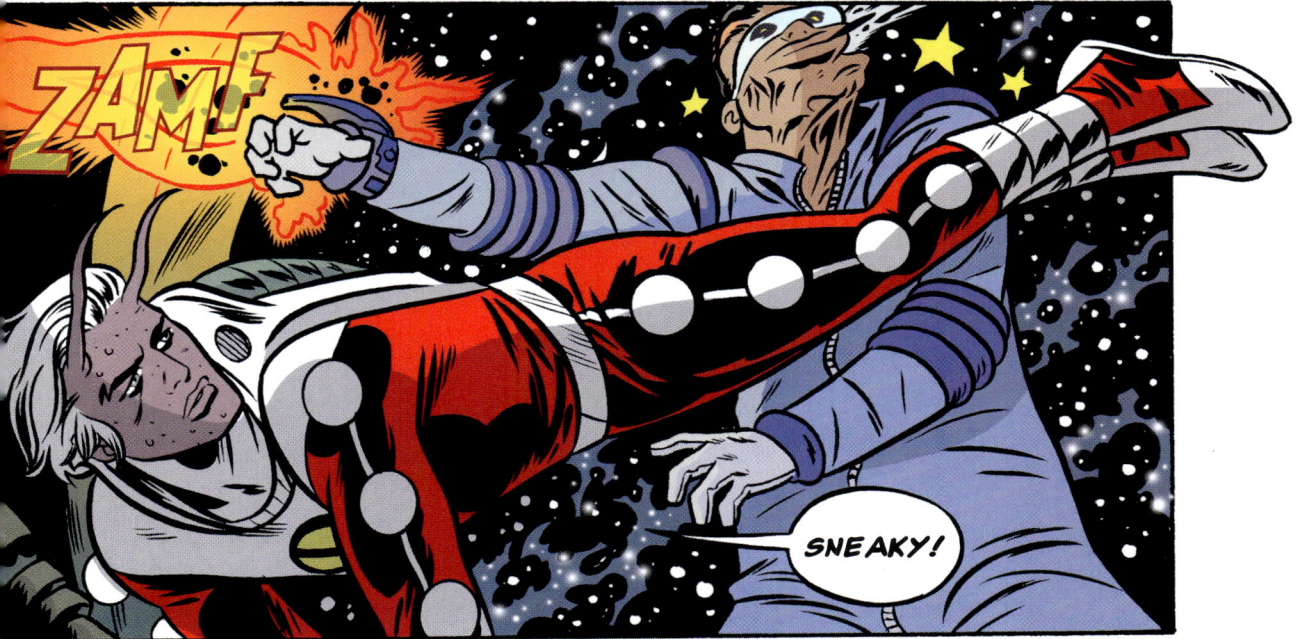

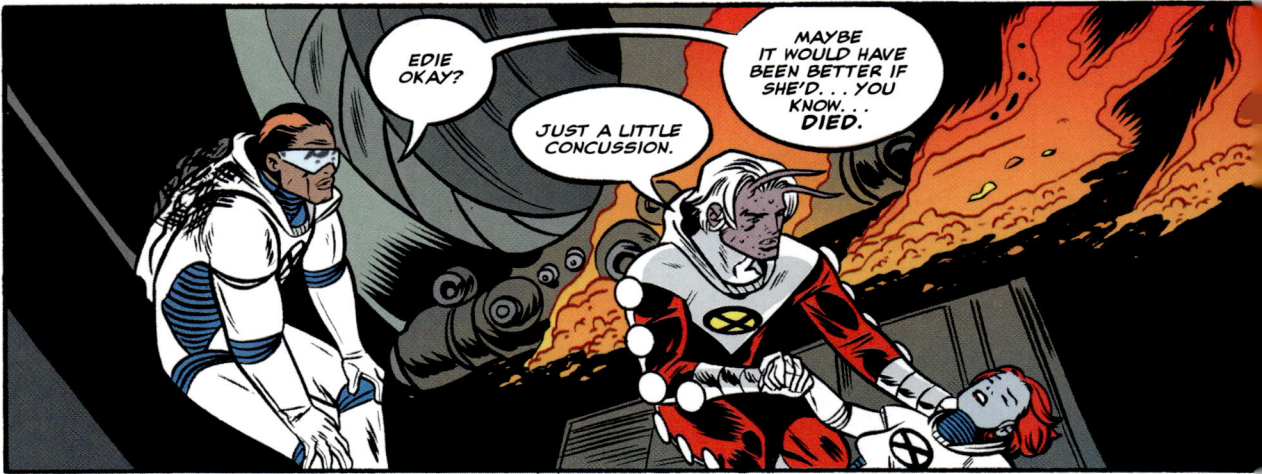

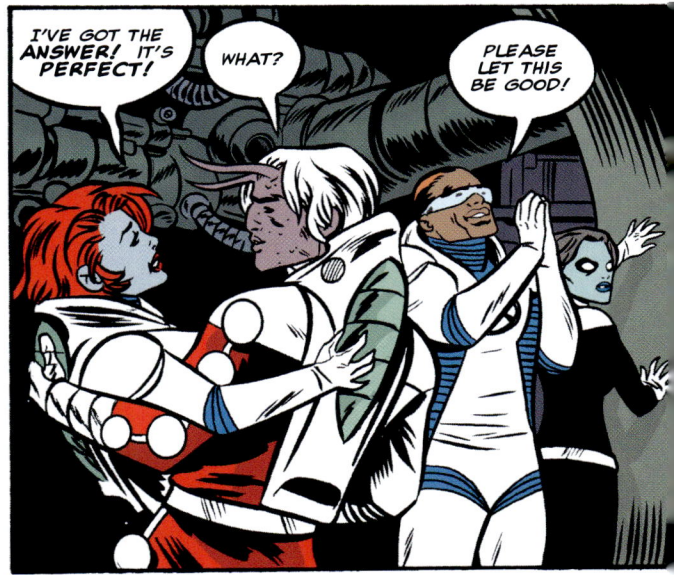

THEY'RE DEAD.

THE MUTANT FIGHTING TEAM KNOWN AS X-FORCE HAS BEEN KILLED BY ALIEN INVADERS.

AT LEAST THAT'S THE WAY IT'S LOOKING.

ARTIST'S RENDITION

THIS IS AN ARTIST'S IMPRESSION OF HOW THINGS MIGHT BE ON THE MARS 2010 SPACE STATION.

BECAUSE THERE'S AN OUTSIDE CHANCE THAT THERE MIGHT BE SURVIVORS UP THERE, A C.I.A. CRACK SQUAD IS ON ITS WAY.

THOUGH IF I WERE YOU, I'D KEEP HOLD OF MY X-FORCE MERCHANDISE... BECAUSE ITS VALUE IS PROBABLY ABOUT TO GO THROUGH THE ROOF.

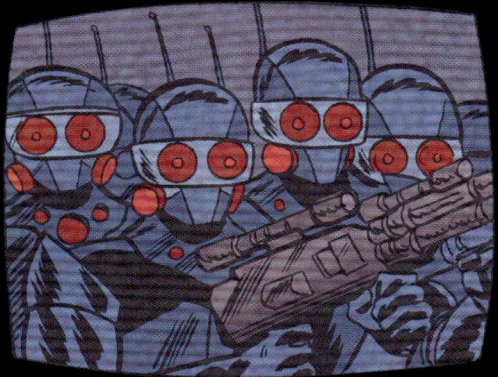

"AND THE WEATHER."

SMITH... CAN YOU HEAR ME?

LOUD AND CLEAR.

WHAT THE HELL ARE YOU DOING? ARE YOU MUTANTS ON VACATION?

JUST SQUEEZING A LITTLE R AND R IN—BETWEEN THE RELENTLESS BLOODSHED AND DRAMA.

YOU LIKE THE SMELL OF ROTTING VEGETATION, DEADGIRL?

X-FORCE CAFE

BECAUSE LOUISE

PETER MILLIGAN—WRITER   MICHAEL ALLRED—ARTIST   LAURA ALLRED—COLORIST

DOC ALLRED & BLAMBOT—LETTERING   JOHN MIESGAES—ASST. EDITOR

AXEL ALONSO—EDITOR   JOE QUESADA—CHIEF   BILL JEMAS—PRESIDENT

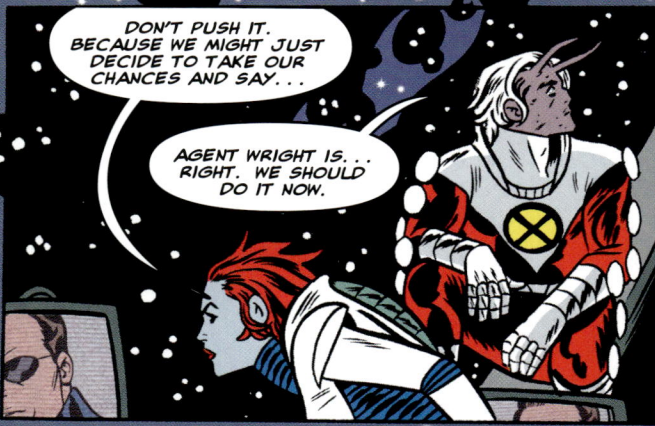

OUR MISSION IS TO LOSE TO A BUNCH OF ALIENS WHO AREN'T REALLY ALIENS...

I DON'T WANT TO BE LIKED. ADORED FROM AFAR. ENVIED. BUT NOT *LIKED.*

AS ALWAYS, THERE ARE COMPLICATIONS.

SOMETIMES IT WOULD BE EASIER IF MY HEARING WASN'T SO *ACUTE.*

I EXPLAINED. I'M IN THE DARK, TOO. WHY ARE YOU SO INTERESTED IN *DEATH?*

IT'S... FORWARD PLANNING. Y' KNOW?

HOW LONG DO WE KEEP THIS UP FOR?

I GUESS WE'RE GONNA HAVE TO... DO STUFF... IN PUBLIC...

UNTIL WE GET MORE RECOGNITION. THEN WE CAN SAY... IT WAS A PHASE. EXPERIMENTATION.

IT MIGHT BE EASIER TO BE LEFT IN THE DARK.

SOME DISPLAYS OF AFFECTION WOULD BE USEFUL. IF YOU THINK YOU COULD MANAGE THAT...

SURE... I MEAN, I GUESS. I MEAN...

SEEING AS WE'RE ONLY *PRETENDING...*

INDULGE IN A LITTLE SELF-DECEPTION.

WHAT?!

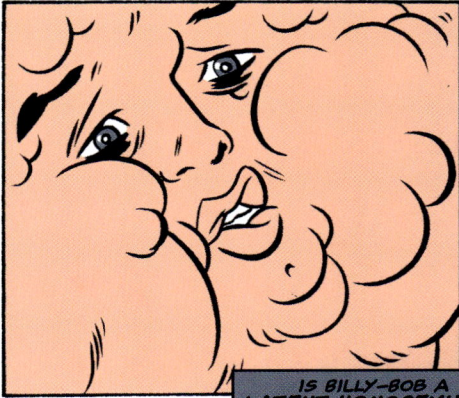

ALL THE BUSH RANGERS ARE DEAD OR WOUNDED BUT THE AMERICAN PUBLIC DON'T NEED TO KNOW THAT. THE OFFICIAL LINE WILL BE THAT YOU *SAVED* US.

CHANGE OF PLAN. THE *OFFICIAL* LINE WILL BE THAT WE *TRIED* TO SAVE YOU.

BUT IN THE HEAT OF BATTLE... THINGS DIDN'T GO QUITE ACCORDING TO PLAN.

X-FORCE ALWAYS DID HAVE A PRETTY HIGH *MORTALITY* RATE.

FOOSH!

ZAM

WHERE THE HELL ARE THEY?

THE CRAFT THAT YOU'RE ON IS HEADED FOR DEEP SPACE.

WE'LL TURN IT AROUND.

IMPOSSIBLE.

YOU'RE IN A COFFIN.

A METAL COFFIN THAT WILL KEEP MOVING THROUGH SPACE UNTIL IT DISINTEGRATES OR COLLIDES WITH SOMETHING VERY SOLID.

BY WHICH TIME, YOU WILL ALL BE LONG DEAD.

TURN US AROUND, WRIGHT! WE PLAYED BALL! THE C.I.A. ARE GONNA COME OUT SMELLIN' OF ROSES.

WHY ARE YOU DOIN' THIS?

BECAUSE...

BECAUSE LOUISE...

BECAUSE MY DAUGHTER, LOUISE, FELL OVER. SHE WAS ONLY THREE SO SHE OFTEN FELL OVER BUT THIS WAS DIFFERENT.

THEY CONDUCTED TESTS AT THE HOSPITAL.

ALL THEY CAN DO IS KEEP HER ALIVE AS LONG AS POSSIBLE AND HOPE THERE'S SOME KIND OF MEDICAL BREAKTHROUGH.

THE KIND OF BREAKTHROUGH PACO PEREZ MIGHT HAVE GIVEN US.

IT'S TOO LATE. THE POPULAR MEMBERS OF X-FORCE ARE AS GOOD AS DEAD.
WE'RE POPULAR. . . JUST IN A DIFFERENT WAY.
AND I HAVEN'T BEEN AROUND LONG ENOUGH TO ESTABLISH MYSELF.
MORE TO THE POINT. . . IF YOU DON'T FIND SOME WAY OF GETTING THEM BACK, WE'RE GOING TO DO SOME VERY UNPOPULAR THINGS TO YOUR NERVOUS SYSTEM.
YOU CAN DO WHAT YOU WANT, THERE'S NOTHING. . .
THUKK
AUUHHGH!

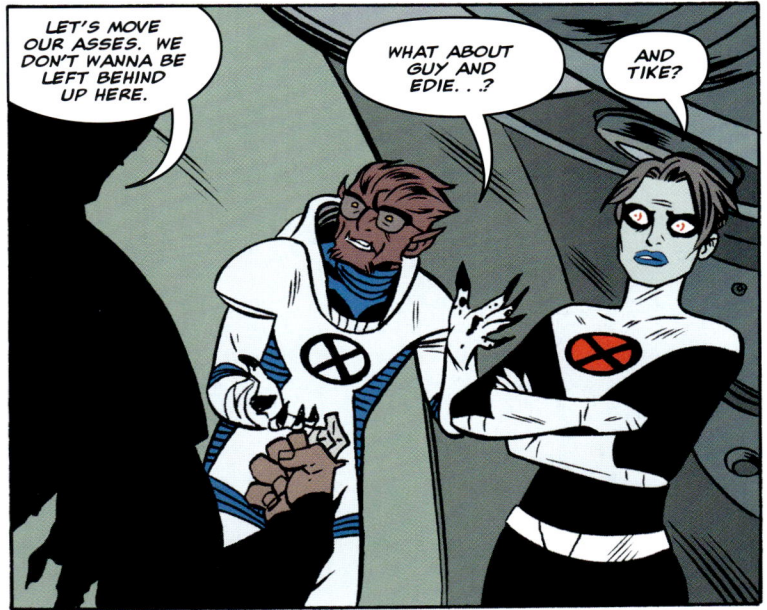

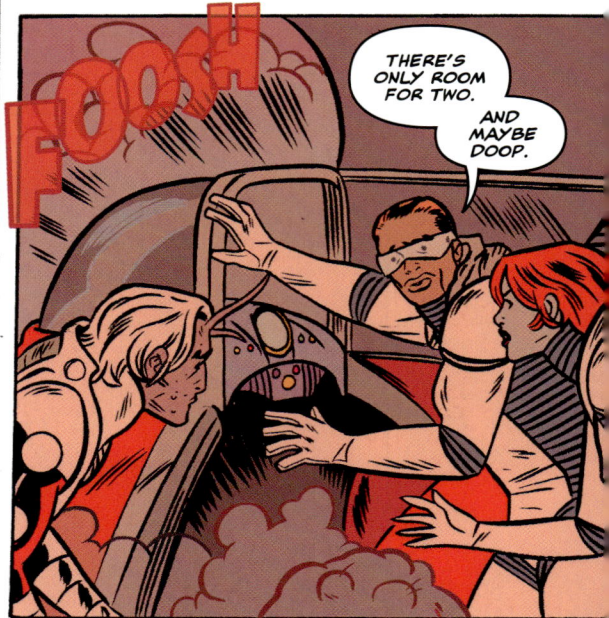

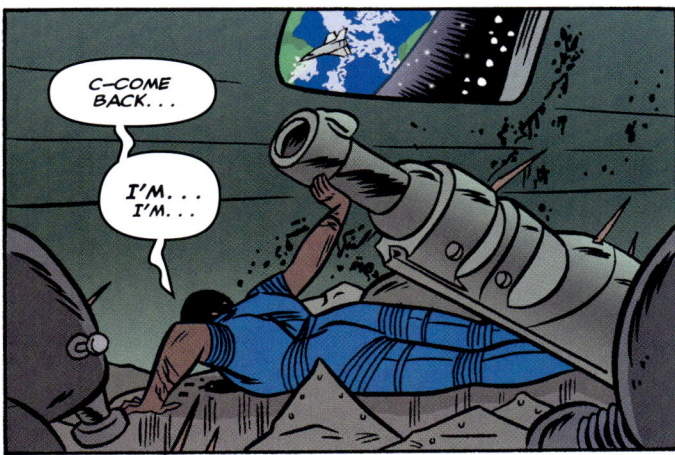

I GUESS WE NEED A *NEW* LEADER.

CAN'T YOU... RECONSTITUTE YOUR MOLECULES IN SOME WAY... TRY TO HEAL YOUR WOUNDS?

I'M TRYING... JUS' SEEMS TO MAKE IT HURT WORSE...

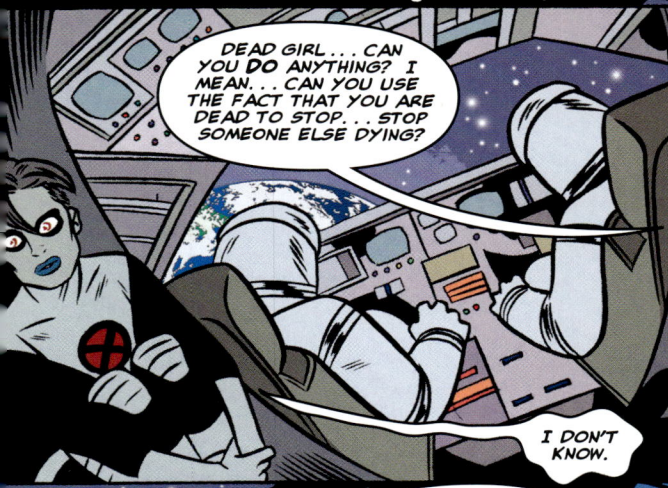

DEAD GIRL... CAN YOU *DO* ANYTHING? I MEAN... CAN YOU USE THE FACT THAT YOU ARE DEAD TO STOP... STOP SOMEONE ELSE DYING?

I DON'T KNOW.

YOU DON'T KNOW? WHAT KIND OF INANE ANSWER IS THAT? WHAT'S THE *POINT* OF YOU, DEAD GIRL?

I SAID... I GUESS WE NEED A NEW LEADER.

GUY, TIKE, AND EDIE AREN'T EVEN *DEAD YET!* AND BILLY BOB IS FIGHTING FOR HIS LIFE...

AND YOU WANT TO HAVE AN *ELECTION?*

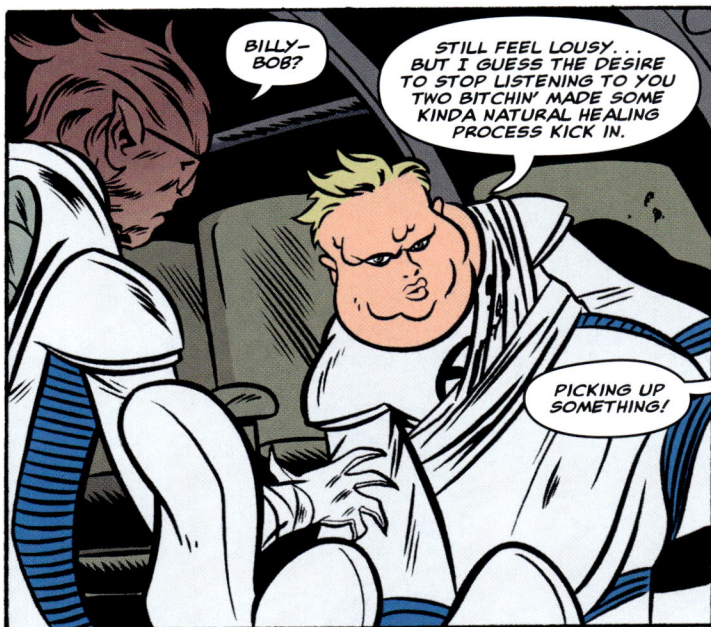

SOMEONE DIES

THERE'S DOOP! OH MY LORD! THERE'RE ONLY **TWO OTHERS!** SOMEONE'S BEEN LEFT BEHIND!

BUT WHO? **WHO?**

PETER MILLIGAN
WRITER

MICHAEL ALLRED
ARTIST

LAURA ALLRED
COLORIST

DOC ALLRED & BLAMBOT
LETTERS

JOHN MIESEGAES
ASST. EDITOR

AXEL ALONSO–EDITOR
JOE QUESADA–CHIEF
BILL JEMAS–PRES.

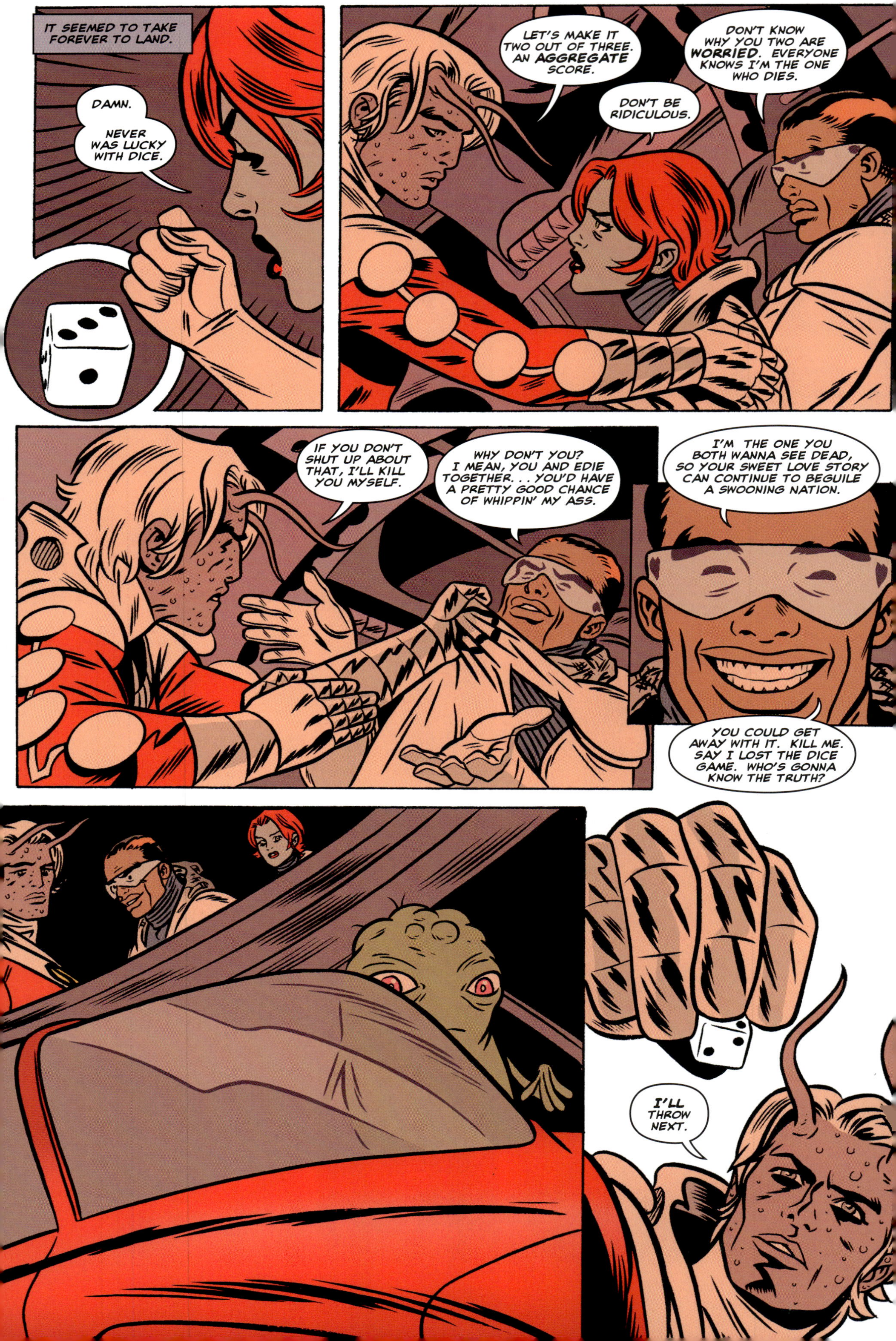
IT SEEMED TO TAKE FOREVER TO LAND.
DAMN.
NEVER WAS LUCKY WITH DICE.
LET'S MAKE IT TWO OUT OF THREE. AN AGGREGATE SCORE.
DON'T KNOW WHY YOU TWO ARE WORRIED. EVERYONE KNOWS I'M THE ONE WHO DIES.
DON'T BE RIDICULOUS.
IF YOU DON'T SHUT UP ABOUT THAT, I'LL KILL YOU MYSELF.
WHY DON'T YOU? I MEAN, YOU AND EDIE TOGETHER. . . YOU'D HAVE A PRETTY GOOD CHANCE OF WHIPPIN' MY ASS.
I'M THE ONE YOU BOTH WANNA SEE DEAD, SO YOUR SWEET LOVE STORY CAN CONTINUE TO BEGUILE A SWOONING NATION.
YOU COULD GET AWAY WITH IT. KILL ME. SAY I LOST THE DICE GAME. WHO'S GONNA KNOW THE TRUTH?
I'LL THROW NEXT.

OR MAYBE A *FIVE.* LESS *OBVIOUS.*

IT WAS EASY FOR GUY AND EDIE. ALL THEY HAD TO DO WAS TRUST IN *LUCK.*

ME, I HAD TO MAKE A *DECISION.*

GOT ENOUGH WATER AND FOOD TO LAST FOUR DAYS, MAYBE A WEEK.

BUT I'M NOT GOING TO HANG AROUND AND DIE ALL SKINNY-ASSED AND DRY-MOUTHED

I STARTED OUT IN THE WHITE SNOW, THE WHITE WORLD OF THE NORTH. GUESS MY WHOLE LIFE HAS BEEN SOME KINDA JOURNEY TO BLACKNESS. *THE SPIKE* WAS PROBABLY RIGHT. I NEVER QUITE MADE IT.

UNTIL NOW.

PRETTY SOON I'LL SUIT-UP AND GO FOR A WALK. JUST LIKE I USED TO GO OUT AND WALK IN THE SNOW...

I'LL KEEP WALKING 'TIL I RUN OUT OF...

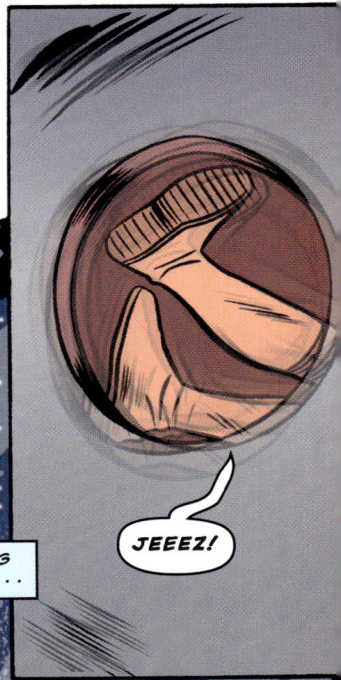

JEEEZ!

UGNNN?

JEEZ... ABDUCTED BY ALIENS.

PLEASE SAY YOU AIN'T GONNA... INTERNALLY INVESTIGATE ME.

WE'RE NOT ALIENS!

AND WE HAVE NO INTENTION OF INVESTIGATING YOU, INTERNALLY OR OTHERWISE.

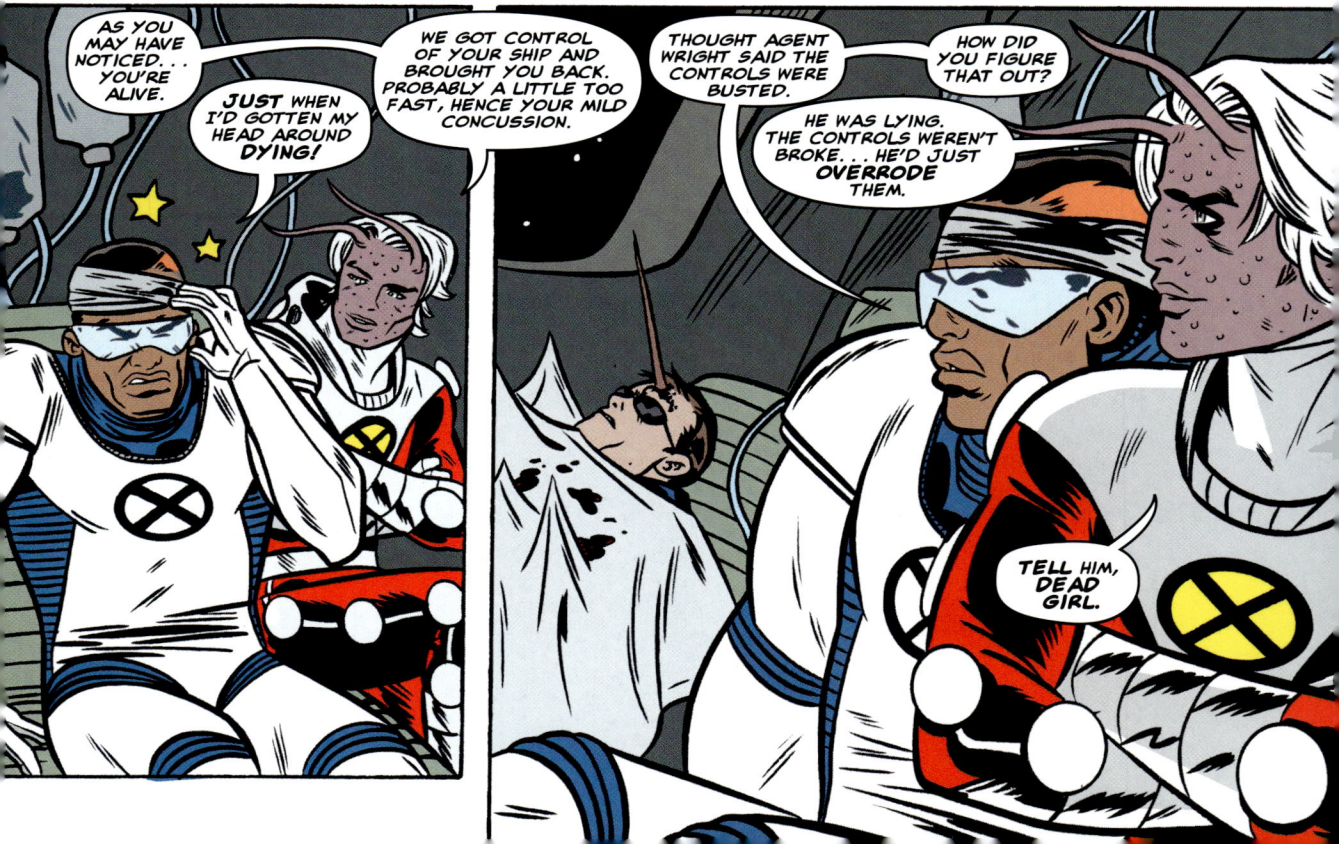

AS YOU MAY HAVE NOTICED... YOU'RE ALIVE.

JUST WHEN I'D GOTTEN MY HEAD AROUND DYING!

WE GOT CONTROL OF YOUR SHIP AND BROUGHT YOU BACK. PROBABLY A LITTLE TOO FAST, HENCE YOUR MILD CONCUSSION.

THOUGHT AGENT WRIGHT SAID THE CONTROLS WERE BUSTED.

HOW DID YOU FIGURE THAT OUT?

HE WAS LYING. THE CONTROLS WEREN'T BROKE... HE'D JUST OVERRODE THEM.

TELL HIM, DEAD GIRL.

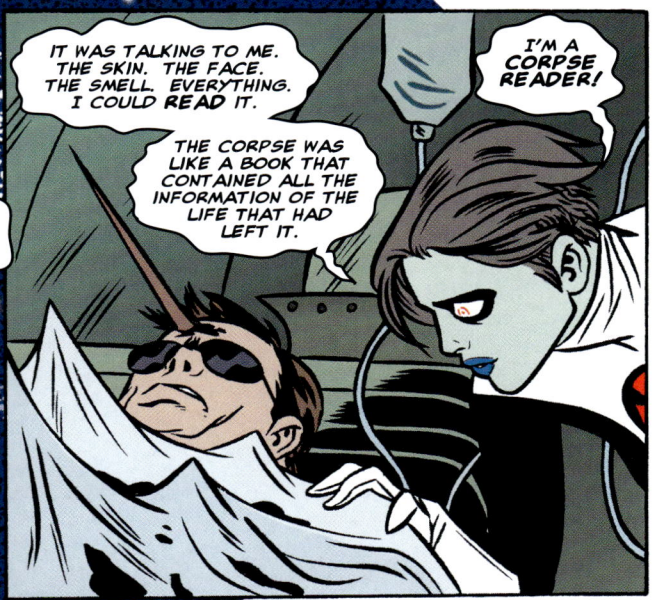

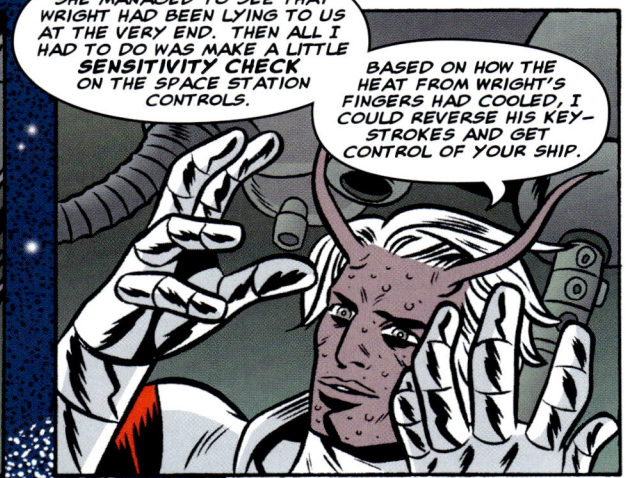

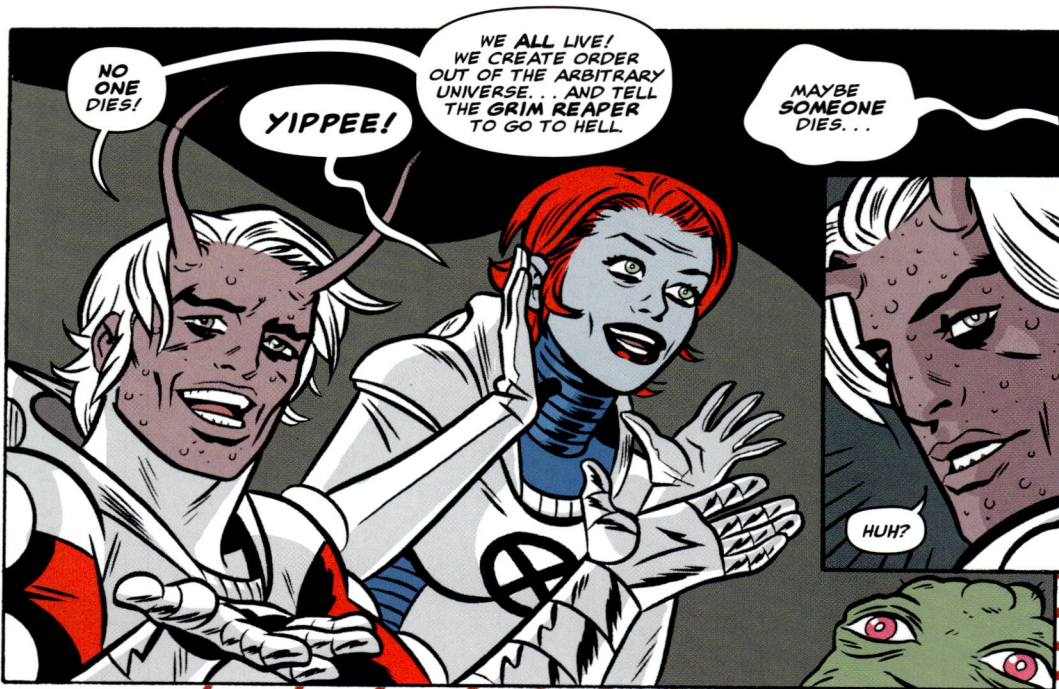

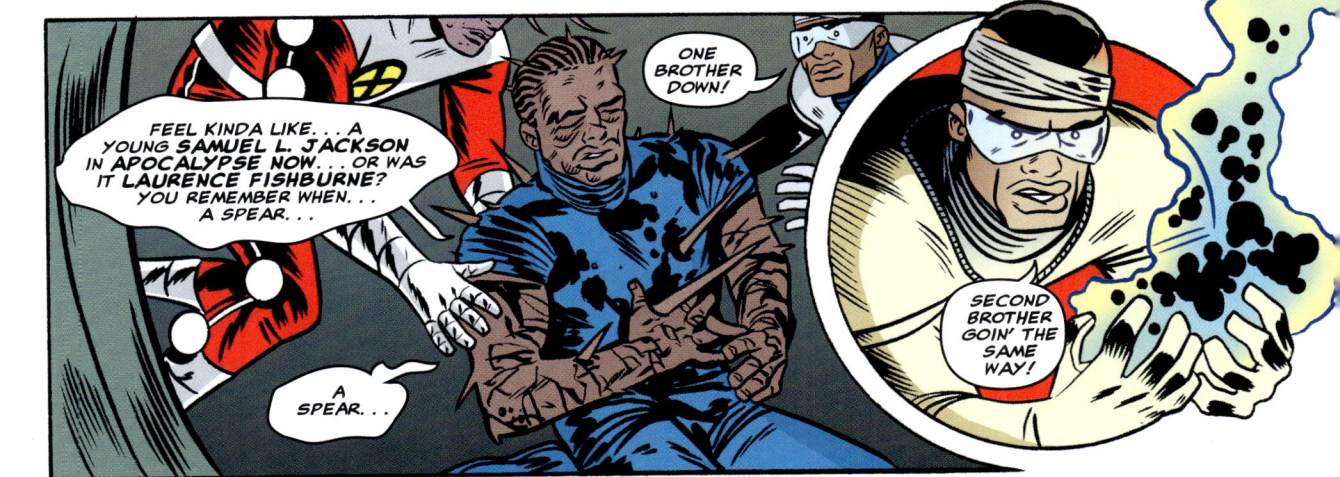

YOU'LL DIE JUST LIKE EVERYONE ELSE, BUSH-RANGER.
DON'T I GET TO HAVE A LAST MEAL BEFORE I'M EXECUTED?
SURE YOU DO.
MY BOOT.
"MY BOOT?" A LITTLE. . . B-MOVIE ACTION HERO, DON'T YOU THINK?
I THOUGHT IT WAS PRETTY COOL, CONSIDERING THE CIRCUMSTANCES.
CASUALTIES?

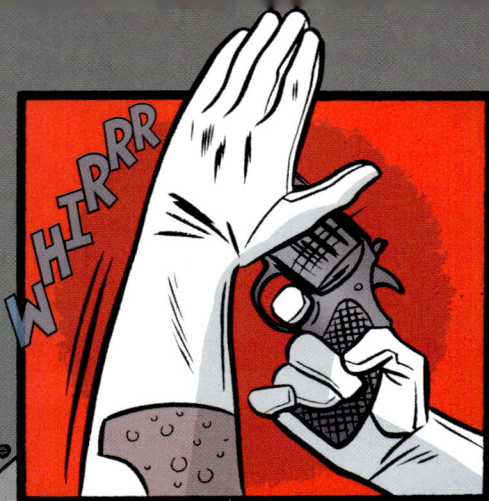

STAN LEE PRESENTS

X STORM!

WRITER
PETER MILLIGAN

ARTIST
DUNCAN FEGREDO

COLORIST
LAURA ALLRED

LETTERER
BLAMBOT'S NATE PIEKOS

ASST. EDITOR
JOHN MIESEGAES

EDITOR
AXEL ALONSO

CHIEF
JOE QUESADA

PRESIDENT
BILL JEMAS

Loyola X-FORCE

THE MOOD OUTSIDE THE *X-FORCE BUILDING* GROWS INCREASINGLY SOMBRE AS RUMORS SPREAD OF THE DEATH OF *EDIE SAWYER*, ALSO KNOWN AS *U-GO GIRL*, PROBABLY THE MOST POPULAR OF ALL X-FORCE MEMBERS.

UNCHARACTERISTICALLY FOR THE NORMALLY MEDIA-FRIENDLY X-FORCE MACHINE, NO OFFICIAL STATEMENT HAS BEEN MADE.

IT *HAS* BEEN CONFIRMED THAT *THE SPIKE* HAS BEEN KILLED IN ACTION, THOUGH *THE SPIKE* HADN'T BEEN AROUND LONG ENOUGH TO CAPTURE THE AMERICAN PUBLIC'S *IMAGINATION.*

AN OBITUARY FOR THE SPIKE CAN BE FOUND ON *WWW. X-FORCE SLASH DECEASED.*

U-GO GIRL

WHAT DO YOU MEAN WE DON'T *TELL* THEM YET? WHY THE HELL NOT?

WE WANT TO BUILD UP THE TENSION. GET EVERYONE TALKING ABOUT IT. IT'S CALLED A *SLOW BURN.* GET THEM WONDERING IF SHE'S GONNA COME BACK.

SO YOU CAN SELL MORE OF *THIS* **CRAP!**

ARE YOU *TRYING* TO BE THE ANTICHRIST OR DOES THIS STUFF COME *NATURAL?*

LIKE IT OR NOT, WE'RE A *BUSINESS.* AND WE'VE GOT A LOT OF *ENEMIES* OUT THERE.

LIKE *WHO?*

X-MEN. X-FACTOR. THE *FANTASTIC FOUR.* YOU NAME 'EM. IT'S A ROUGH, COMPETITIVE MARKETPLACE.

I CAN'T... I MEAN... I CAN'T REALLY *BELIEVE* WHAT'S *HAPPENED*...

I *KNOW* HOW YOU FEEL. IT GOES AGAINST THE GRAIN FOR ME BUT... I'M TRYING NOT TO THINK ABOUT IT. TRYING NOT TO *ANALYZE* IT. I'M JUST LETTING THINGS --

ACTUALLY, I WAS TALKING ABOUT *EDIE.*

YOU MEAN... WHAT'S HAPPENED WITH US... IS JUST AN EVERYDAY, TOTALLY PREDICTABLE OCCURRENCE?

I MEAN... I CAN'T GET MY HEAD AROUND *ANYTHING* ANYMORE. EDIE DYING. EDIE OF ALL PEOPLE. MAKES YOU FEEL...

MORTAL?

THE GREEKS WOULD HAVE SAID THAT SHE HAD A GOOD *DEATH.* IN HER PRIME. DOING WHAT SHE DID BEST.

IN LOVE.

BUT *TOO SOON. WAY* TOO SOON.

THEN WHAT'S THE *ANSWER?* TO CUT YOURSELF OFF FROM ALL THAT? TO CAUTERIZE YOUR HEART?

I DON'T KNOW. I'M JUST THE GUY WHO CAN DO WEIRD THINGS WITH HIS FAT. *YOU'RE* THE CLEVER ONE.

I *WISH.*

"GUY! GUY, CAN YOU TELL US..."

"CAN YOU GIVE US ANY NEWS ON *EDIE?*"

MRS. SAWYER... WHEN DID YOU LEARN OF YOUR DAUGHTER'S DEATH?
HOW DO YOU *FEEL?*
WHEN'S THE LAST TIME YOU *SPOKE* TO HER?
PLEASE... I DON'T...
PLEASE, JUST...
PLEASE...
BACK OFF! GIVE THE LADY SOME ROOM! FOR GOD'S SAKE, HAVE NONE OF YOU ANY SHAME?
MRS. SAWYER HAS NOTHING TO SAY AT THE MOMENT.
SHE MAY BE GIVING SELECTIVE INTERVIEWS AT A LATER DATE WHEN SHE'S MORE COMPOSED. *THESE* CAN BE ARRANGED THROUGH MY OFFICE.
FOR THOSE OF YOU WHO'VE BEEN LIVING ON MARS FOR THE LAST FEW MONTHS, I'M *SOLOMON O'SULLIVAN.*
I'LL BE REPRESENTING MRS. SAWYER'S INTERESTS FROM NOW ON.

I DON'T THINK... I MEAN... WE'RE JUST NORMAL PEOPLE, MR. SULLIVAN.
THERE ARE NO SUCH THINGS AS NORMAL OR ABNORMAL PEOPLE! JUST PEOPLE WHO THE MEDIA ARE OR ARE NOT INTERESTED IN.
YOU ARE NOW INTERESTING. BUT WITHOUT PROFESSIONAL HELP, THEY'LL EAT YOU UP AND SPIT YOU OUT AND YOU'LL END WITH NOTHING.
I HAVE NO INTENTION OF MAKING... A PROFIT OUT OF EDIE'S DEATH.
THAT'S VERY COMMENDABLE, MRS. SAWYER, BUT DO YOU THINK X-FORCE HAS THE SAME HIGH MORAL STANDARDS?
THE HELL THEY DO! THEY'RE MAKING A MINT. AND HAVE THEY CONTACTED YOU? HAVE YOU HAD A WORD FROM THEM?
NO...
DON'T YOU THINK YOUR DAUGHTER, GOD REST HER SOUL, DON'T YOU THINK SHE WOULD HAVE WANTED YOU, HER OWN MOTHER, TO BENEFIT FROM THIS TRAGIC EVENT?
OF COURSE SHE WOULD HAVE.
I KNOW WHAT I'M DOING. I'M SOLOMON O'SULLIVAN. FIFTY PER CENT JEWISH. FIFTY PER CENT IRISH.
ONE HUNDRED PER-CENT BEHIND YOU.

"POLICE SAY THAT NO CHARGES WILL BE MADE AGAINST THE X-FORCERS, BUT IT'S *RUMORED* THAT TIKE WILL MAKE A LARGE DONATION TO THE L.A.P.D BENEVOLENT FUND.

CMP

CMP

10 10

LAM 22

"THOUGH FREELANCE PHOTOGRAPHER ED LANCE HAS REPORTEDLY FILED A CIVIL ACTION AGAINST ALICAR FOR CRIMINAL DAMAGE AND EMOTIONAL TRAUMA.

"THIS IS X-FORCE NEWS AT..."

TIKE AND DEAD GIRL.

MAYBE THEY'RE MAKING A PLAY AT BEING THE NEW *GOLDEN COUPLE.*

CLKK

YOUR MARKETING TEAM SHOULD BE ABLE TO RUN WITH THAT.

I ASKED YOU... I *TOLD* YOU... NOT TO TELL THEM ABOUT EDIE.

AND I DID. SO WHAT'RE YOU GOING TO DO ABOUT IT, SPIKE? FIRE ME? *FINE* ME A WEEK'S WAGES?

I COULD MAKE SOME CALLS TO THOSE DRUG COMPANIES... TELL THEM TO GO AHEAD WITH THOSE COMMERCIALS... "GUY SMITH: THE MAN WHO GAVE AWAY PACO PEREZ"... AND WITH IT THE CHANCE TO DEFEAT ANY NUMBER OF TERMINAL DISEASES!

YOU THINK I CARE? DO YOU THINK I GIVE A DAMN IF I'M THE MOST HATED MAN IN THE WORLD? GO AHEAD. I DON'T GIVE A DAMN!

GET YOURSELF CLEANED UP BY TOMORROW. WE'RE VISITING SOME FARM TEAMS. LOOKING AT REPLACE-MENTS. IT'S OPEN TO THE MEDIA MAYBE WE CAN SALVAGE SOMETHING FROM THIS MESS.

WHAT ARE WE DOING HERE? DON'T WE USUALLY JUST LOOK AT THEIR REELS?
FREEMAN THINKS IT'S GOOD FOR P.R..
SHOW THE WORLD WE'RE STILL A TEAM.
JEEZ!
SPLISH
WHO OR WHAT IN THE NAME OF EVERYTHING HOLY IS THAT?
APPARENTLY OPERATES UNDER THE NAME OF... WASH-OUT.
"A CHRONIC CHILD BED-WETTER WHO ONE FINE DAY MANAGED TO HARNESS THE POWER OF HIS NOCTURNAL OUTPOURINGS AND USE THEM AGAINST THE TYRANNICAL POLY-GAMOUS SECT IN WHICH HE WAS RAISED."

VENUS DEE MILO IS ON A MISSION. WE CAN CHECK OUT HER REEL LATER.

MY NAME'S SOLOMON O'SULLIVAN.

I'M SPECIALIZING IN MUTANTS AND RELATED MATTERS. THOUGHT YOU SHOULD KNOW THAT I NOW REPRESENT QUITE A FEW OF THE LIKELY-LADS YOU'VE BEEN WATCHING TODAY.

VENUS DEE MILO IS WITH ME, TOO.

MAYBE. MAYBE YOU CAN CHECK OUT HER REEL LATER.

I LOOK OUT FOR MY CLIENTS. JUS' BECAUSE YOU HAVE AN UNCANNY SUPER POWER DON'T MEAN YOU KNOW YOUR WAY AROUND A LEGAL CONTRACT.

I NEGOTIATE TERMS AND CONDITIONS. IMAGE RIGHTS. SO ON.

WE'VE ALREADY GOT AGENTS.

AGENTS WHO DON'T UNDERSTAND YOU. AGENTS WHO AIN'T GOT THE FIRST IDEA WHAT IT'S LIKE TO BE... DIFFERENT.

AND YOU DO?

IT STARTED WHEN I WAS NINETEEN.

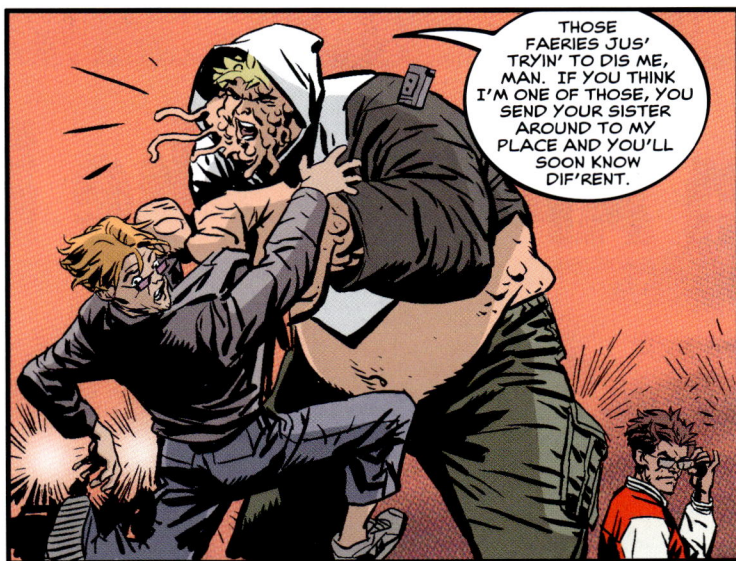

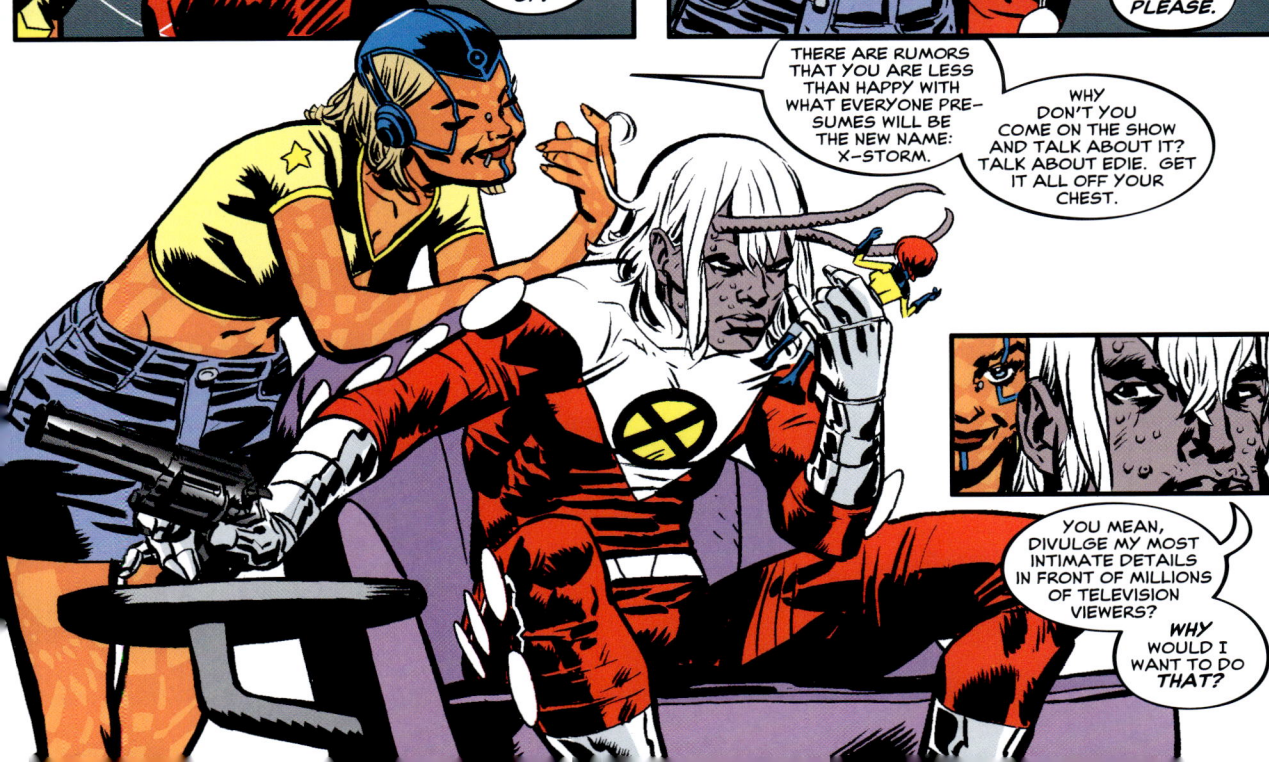

AND... THEN EDIE... SHE WHISPERED...

"X-STATIX."

AREN'T YOU GOING TO SAY SOME-THING?

I GUESS YOU COULD SAY... IT WAS HER *DYING WISH.*

'BOUT *WHAT?*

LET'S SEE...

LACUNA and the STARS

PERHAPS YOU COULD OUTLINE YOUR VIEWS ON THE INFLUENCE OF *THE REFORM-ATION* ON *MODERN ART.*

OR *MAYBE* YOU'D LIKE TO TELL ME WHY YOU CAME OUT WITH THAT COWARDLY, NASTY *HOMOPHOBIC BULL!*

I DON'T WANT... EVERY-ONE KNOWING ABOUT IT.

THAT WAS THE IDEA... WHEN WE WERE *PRE-*TENDING!

BUT THAT WAS THE *IDEA!*

ISN'T THAT THE REASON? THAT YOU'VE NEVER DONE IT WITH A *DEAD GIRL* BEFORE! I WANT TO BE MORE THAN JUST NOVELTY VALUE, TIKE!

YOU *ARE!*

I DON'T *BELIEVE* YOU!

MAYBE WE *ALL* NEED A LITTLE HELP.

AND NOW I DECLARE THE *DOOP KIDDIES HOSPITAL* OPEN.

AND FINALLY I WANT TO SAY THAT WHATEVER MAY HAVE HAPPENED... WHATEVER YOU MAY HAVE HEARD... WHOEVER WE MIGHT HAVE *LOST*...

WE'RE HERE TODAY TO SHOW THE WORLD THAT WE ARE STILL A *TEAM*.

KIDDIES

64

...WE'VE GOT NO TENSIONS OR IN-FIGHTING...

...NO BAD BLOOD...

...BUT WE *DO* HAVE A NEW NAME.

FROM THIS MOMENT ON, THE TEAM FORMERLY KNOWN AS *X-FORCE* WILL BE KNOWN AS...

THE END.

X-FORCE
Sketchbook

Doodled while chatting with series editor Axel Alonso, these thumbnail sketches are Mike Allred's first concepts for the new X-Force.

FLAX ①
MARX ②
③
④
DE MILO (VENUS?) ⑤
⑥
DOOP
⑦ THE ANARCHIST
⑧
⑨
BLAK
⑩
⑪
TORK
⑫ GO GIRL GO GO VENUS THERD
⑬
⑭
PLAZM
⑮
⑯
⑰
⑱
⑲
⑳
DEAD GUY
㉑
㉒
㉓ THE ORPHAN
JELLYFISH
㉔
㉕ ROBBY RODRIGUEZ
HOOK

SPORT
FLAK
TIKE
STUD

The individual character designs begin to coalesce as Mike nails down costumes and color schemes for the main cast.

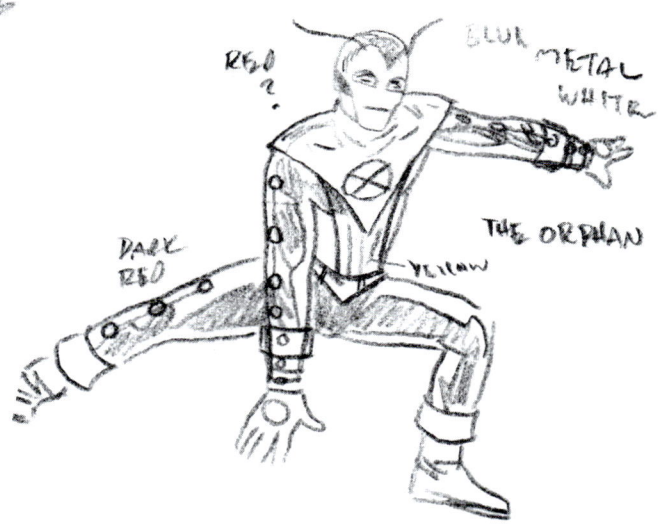

DOOP
GREEN

DEE MILO
WIG BLUE/BLACK HAIR
RED FACE
YELLOW

SENTINEL PURPLE

AXEL PLAZM

DARK TAN

RED?

BLUE METAL WHITE

THE ORPHAN

DARK RED

YELLOW

PURPLE/BLACK SKIN

YELLOW BLUE

TRYING YOGA TO CHILL HOT TEMPER

TIKE ALICIA
THE ANARCHIST

"FRANZ" SKIN

PALE BLUE OR WHITE SKIN

RED HAIR

BLUE GREEN TURQUOISE

GO-GO GIRL

The team takes center stage in this inked sketch, including the X-Force headquarters.

Two potential team lineups emerge!

Mike's talent knows no end! The Renaissance man straps down the *X-Force* logo design.

THE ASTOUNDING
X-FORCE

I DID THIS ONE JUST FOR FUN...

X-FORCE

X-FORCE

BUT I LIKE THIS ONE BIG-TIME--
BOLD, SIMPLE, CLASSIC AND FUNKY!

X-FORCE

THE ALL-NEW, ALL-DIFFERENT
X-FORCE

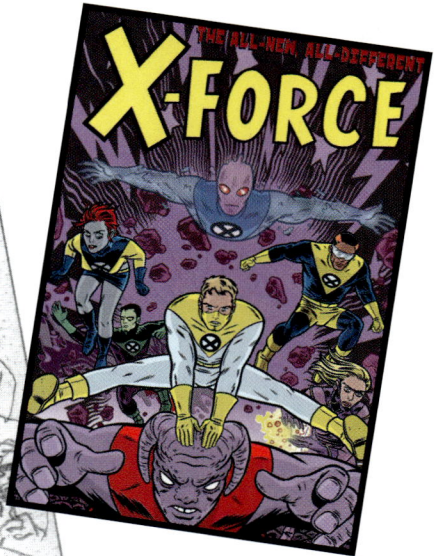

X-Force #116 cover thumbnail sketch.

X-Force #116 alternate cover colors by Laura Allred.

Mike's original cover sketch for *X-Force #120,* and the final cover (inset).

Unpublished Cover: Heavily influenced by comics visionary Jim Steranko, this cover was the first full-color depiction of the original X-Force team.

Unpublished Cover: This cover shows X-Force in action wearing their nighttime battle gear.

Mike Allred's concepts for the first *X-Force* trade paperback cover.

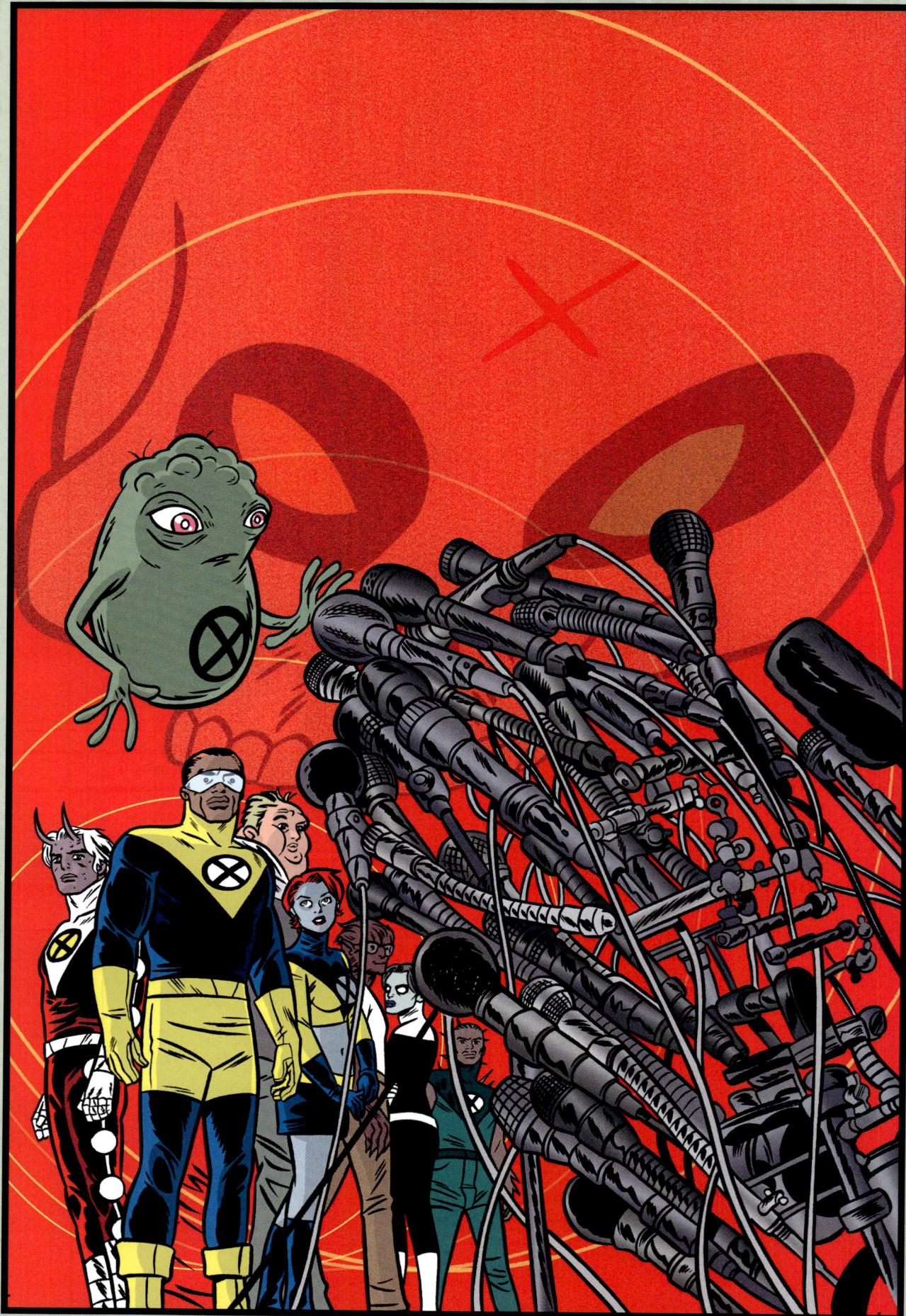

Watch out on the dance floor! Doop cuts a mean rug from the X-Force screensaver.

X-Force's star-crossed couple in a pin-up by Darwyn Cooke.

Darwyn Cooke drew these pin-ups of X-Force heartthrobs Guy Smith and Edie Sawyer as Christmas gifts for Mike and Laura Allred.

Darwyn Cooke's U-Go Girl
pin-up for Axel Alonso and
an unused Anarchist pin-up.

X-FORCE

ISSUE #123
WRITER: PETER MILLIGAN
ARTIST: MICHAEL ALLRED
COLORS: LAURA ALLRED

'NUFF SAID

Right. Have we got a title for this yet? If not, I'd like to call it TICK TOCK because all the action takes place within the elongated architecture of a second, or at least the time it takes for the second hand of a clock to travel from the land of Tick to the far off environs of Tock.

PAGE ONE

1. We're in the main living area of X-Force HQ. Nice big shot taking up top half of the page of our team having a little R and R. TV, books, whatever. As long as it isn't good for the mind.

I'd like you to put in some prominent position a clock with some kind of recognizable face. Maybe it's an authentic X-FORCE CLOCK (available at all good stores now!) because this clock and time itself will play an important part in what we might laughingly term this month's story.

But what's this?

Doop is in the corner of the room. Its back to us. What's going on? Is Doop sulking?

2. Nope. Close on Doop. Like a lot of stunted green blob creatures of indeterminate gender, Doop sometimes suffers from skin that is both dry and greasy, leading to embarrassing ZITS. And usually they spring up right before a party, or a battle against superhuman tyrants.

So right here we're close to Doop who is floating in front of a MIRROR and is about to — yes, we've all done it, Jesus, even the Queen has probably done it (or at least got a lady-in-waiting to do it for her!) – Doop's about to squeeze the puss out of that bad boy.

3. CLOSE DETAIL OF THE CLOCK. Let's say it is one second to noon. The second hand moving.

WE ART IN SFX: TICK

4. AND NOW A VERY CLOSE SHOT OF DOOP…Eyes show alarm as it wonders just what it's about to squeeze out…

PAGE TWO AND THREE

Right. I'd like one of those nice big double-page spreads now.

My god. X-Force has faced some tough tests but none like this. To the left of the spread we see Doop. It's squeezed its spot.

But what is radiating from it is like nothing on earth. It is a tsunami of reality-bending, dimensional-challenging weirdness, blowing through and blowing away the assorted members of X-FORCE…whose weird and hallucinatory trajectory takes them right across into the second page of this spread…

Make this pretty heavy too. These guys are really being blown away.

ROLL TITLE AND CREDITS: TICK TOCK

Peter Milligan – Writer, Mike Allred – Artist, Etc.

PAGE FOUR

1. Doop looks at the room. It's an X-Force Marie Celeste. All the food and books and TVs or whatever it was that the guys were doing is just as it was. But there is no sign of any of X-Force.

2. CLOSE on Doop. Hand over its mouth. Oops!

3. It looks at its reflection in the mirror. The little cavity where the zit has been squeezed.

And has an idea. It might be a long shot but what is there to lose (besides our entire readership)?

4. CLOSE. Doop is working a FINGER right INTO THE ZIT HOLE!

PAGE FIVE

1. Right. And now things start to get a little strange. We seem now to be INSIDE DOOP. We can see its finger and part of its hand coming in through the zit hole.

2. Cut back to outside… and the process is continuing. Doop now has an arm in through the enlarged zit hole.

3. CUT BACK Inside Doop. Incredibly, one of its eyes can be seen coming in through the zit hole. The plucky little creature is somehow turning itself outside in…WE SHOULD SEE THE STRAIN AND EFFORT THIS IS PUTTING THE LITTLE DOOP THROUGH.

4. Cut back outside as Doop DISAPPEARS INTO ITSELF… maybe just a shimmer or a ghost image of where Doop was… the X FORCE CLOCK SHOULD BE SEEN ON THE WALL…

5. CLOSE ON THE CLOCK. The time is the same… the second hand still has not moved…

PAGE SIX

1. WE'RE NOW INSIDE "DOOP LAND." And it is a strange place indeed. And pretty horrific. A kind of Doop sensibility meets Hieronymos Bosch. A huge vista spreads out before Doop. And it seems to be teeming with millions – or an artistic approximation thereof – of Doop-like creatures. But these are strange misshapen Doops. These are Doops from the dark side of the id.

2. On Doop. Biting its nails or showing some other sign of trepidation.

3. Then it looks up. High above is the zit hole… through which the clock – set at the same time – hovers like a strange orbiting planet.

PAGE SEVEN

1. CUT. We seem to be in some kind of INNER CITY. Some poor run-down area. There are a lot of YOUNG BLACK GUYS coming towards us. This can be pretty hallucinatory...dark...these guys are definitely threatening...

2. Pull back...we see that PHAT is here. But he isn't seeing these guys as his brothers. He is scared witless by them. Backing away...

3. He turns and runs...

4. But now there are more BLACK PEOPLE coming the other way. Make it nightmarish. The dark night, the shadows, and the black people merging into one...

PAGE EIGHT

1. CUT BACK TO DOOP. This can be pretty violent. Doop is trying to wade its way through the legions of EVIL DOOPS.

2. Up ahead he sees a kind of WINDOW or SCREEN. Maybe like a segment from a stained glass window. On it we see Phat's scared face. Doop is trying to get to it.

3. AN EVIL DOOP SINKS ITS TEETH INTO DOOP'S ARM. Doop screaming in pain...

4. And then thuds its finger in the evil Doop's eye...making it let go...

5. It leaps towards the tortured image of Phat...

PAGE NINE

1. Here we see DOOP arriving in the nightmare ghetto land that Phat has found himself in. Doop is a giant here, looming over Phat and the fleeing black guys...

2. Doop grabs Phat in its hand...like a little green King Kong...

3. And now Doop pops Phat screaming into its mouth!

PAGE TEN

1. CUT. We retain our nightmarish theme.

We're in a kind of Borgesian, Escher-like LIBRARY. Long dark corridors leading back into terrible nothingness.

Myles is pulling books off the shelves. He's going crazy... there should be some books open around him.

2. We see why. He's holding TWO BOOKS. All the pages are blank. If we could we should see more books with blank pages all around him... MYLES IS CLIMBING UP THE SIDE OF THE SHELVES TO REACH SOME HIGHER BOOKS...

3. And now the books collapse around him as he falls... the empty pages like dry leaves fluttering about him...

4. From the pile of blank books that swamp him he looks up... from the corridor comes some STRANGE giant demon VERSION OF HIS FATHER. WITH A CANE. DEAD EYES. HE IS NAKED. AND THERE IS WRITING... INDECIPHERABLETEXT... IN DOOP LANGUAGE MAYBE... SCRAWLED ALL OVER HIM...

PAGE ELEVEN

1. Myles screams silently and tries to clamber out of the books. The figure of the father-monster is gaining on him.

2. CLOSE on Myles...seeing a book in front of him... DOOP is on the cover...

3. Weird shot as Myles opens the page and something HUGE SHOOTS OUT OF IT...

4. It's DOOP. Like a POP-OUT DOOP from the Doop book. Looming above Myles...

5. Doop sucks in...and sucks in Myles...him...

PAGE TWELVE

1. It's DOOP now in the library. Myles has gone. Doop is looking down curiously at one of the BOOKS lying in the pile around it.

2. It picks it up and we see the cover. "SPIKEY CROSS-DRESSING." And on the cover a big pic of THE SPIKE dressed in women's clothes. Let's make this very sexy and very strange.

3. Doop looks around. This gets worse. Or better, depending on your politics.

LOTS OF TINY DOOPS DRESSED AS WOMEN ARE CHARGING DOWN THE CORRIDOR TOWARDS HIM.

WE SHOULD SEE THE CLOCK IN THE 'SKY' ABOVE...

4. DOOP'S POV: THE CLOCK, STILL SHOWING one second to noon but it's almost as though we see the second hand twitching as it tries eagerly to move to tock...

5. On Doop. What the hell? It tosses the Spikey Cross Dressing book into its mouth with a kind of "what else can a Doop do?: shrug...or as close as someone with Doop's physiognomy can get to shrugging.

PAGE THIRTEEN

1. CUT. A desert scene. Desert full of scorched bones, Dali-esque skeletons. There are A NUMBER OF BURNING SUNS IN THE SKY. And there is a figure — dark, we can't make him out — crawling towards us...

2. CLOSE ON THIS FIGURE. It's TIKE. He seems in a bad way. Burning up. THE SWEAT IS DRIPPING MADLY OFF OF HIM...but his face is bloated, as though there's a lot more fluid almost bursting to come out...

3. He looks down at his hands: the SWEAT IS FLOWING FROM HIS PALMS LIKE WATER, steaming...hot sweat...

4. We pull back and now we see him EXPLODING IN A BALL OF WARM SWEAT

PAGE FOURTEEN

1. NOW THE DESERT has been transformed into a vile, sweaty sea...a sea of sweat and phlegm and bodily excretions... and Tike is drowning in it... gasping... waving his tired arms helplessly out...

2. We move UNDER THE SEA OF SWEAT with Tike as he sinks ... drowning in the awful sludge...

3. But now...what's this? He sees DOOP swimming powerfully towards him... Tike's eyes wide with surprise and hope...

PAGE FIFTEEN

1. CUT. We are in a huge room: all stainless steel and sharp edges. Clinical, a nightmarish warped OPERATING THEATER. Around the side of the room are some kind of TRANSPARENT PLINTHS. Each contains some thing we cannot make out yet. In the middle of the room, small, vulnerable, her back to us, is a figure we recognize as Edie. She seems to have her hands to her face.

2. We move up to and around Edie and see that her hands are over her mouth. Something is wrong. Her eyes show pain and confusion. THERE IS BLOOD TRICKLING FROM IN-BETWEEN HER FINGERS.

3. Edie drops her hands. Dark blood is coming from her mouth...

PAGE SIXTEEN

1. She crawls over to one of the weird transparent plinths. Inside it, suspended in the glass...is a grisly sight. A SEVERED TONGUE!

2. But now she looks down at the other plinths and we see that each one contains a severed tongue. Some fatter. Some redder. But each one a tongue. We are in the HALL OF TONGUES!

3. Going crazy...she runs down the rows of severed tongues. She's looking for her tongue! Where is it?

4. Up ahead...she sees a familiar figure, atop a plinth. It's Doop. Beckoning her towards it...

PAGE SEVENTEEN

1. Edie reaches the plinth with Doop, who points down to the tongue held inside it. She's smiling! She'd know her own tongue anywhere...

2. Doop hits the plinth, which shatters...Edie is catching her tongue...

3. CLOSE on Edie pushing her tongue back into her mouth...

4. CLOSE A smiling Edie – tongue in place, and we can see it – goes to talk, but...

5. CLOSE Doop. Finger to its mouth. Shhh!

PAGE EIGHTEEN

A BIG DRAMATIC FULL PAGED SHOT featuring the only member of our crew we haven't seen yet.

Guy Smith.

But Guy – and I have a feeling that this won't come as a complete surprise to you – Guy is in trouble. He is buried up to his neck. And he is screaming. Face distorting with acute pain.

BECAUSE THERE ARE WHAT APPEAR TO BE INSECTS, crawling all over his face... he's powerless to get them off...

We should be far enough away not to be able to completely discern what kind of insects these are...

PAGE NINETEEN

1. CLOSER. And we see that these are not insects that are tormenting Guy but hundreds of tiny evil DEMON DOOPS. Biting, stabbing, scratching... in Guy's nostrils... getting into his eyes...his mouth... his eyes are slits... he's trying to open them...

2. A SHADOW FALLS OVER GUY'S FACE. He opens his pained eyes and looks up...

3. Reverse angle – looking up so we see that Doop – the real non-demon Doop – is looming above Guy...

4. PULL AROUND. Doop has taken hold of Guy's head and is pulling at it with all its might trying to pull Guy out of the ground...

PAGE TWENTY

1. And something gives... Doop falls back...

2. Eeek! Doop has Guy's DECAPITATED HEAD in its hands. Staring at it. Guy doesn't seem to be pained by being decapitated. He seems to be looking at Doop with something like gratitude. What a guy!

3. Doop looks around. There's THE CLOCK...second hand twitching...and also the APERTURE through which Doop entered Doop World.

4. Doop tucks Guy under its arm football-style and runs like a line back towards the aperture...

PAGE TWENTY-ONE

1. BACK TO HQ. Doop appears, in mid-air, emerging from itself, as though righting itself after being turned inside out...the clock is right next to it...

2. Doop – now fully formed and normal sticks a finger against the second hand, stopping its normal passage...WE SEE THAT DOOP'S ZIT, the one that started all the trouble, looks huge and full of puss. Its other hand is about to squeeze it again...

3. WHOOSH! It all comes out. A blurred, amorphous puss-like amalgam of THE X-FORCE TEAM... spurting in a blurred mass from Doop's zit...

PAGE TWENTY-TWO

1. X-Force reform in the HQ. THEY SHOULD BE IN EXACTLY THE SAME POSITION THAT THEY WERE IN just before Doop blew them all away by squeezing the poison from its zit.

2. Doop looks up at the clock. Finally the second hand flips over and the clock goes...

TOCK

3. Doop smiles at us in relief. Phew!

And the annoying zit seems to have vanished.

THE END

Dedications

"For everyone I've ever met who was nice to me."
Mike Allred

"For everyone I've ever met who was horrible to me."
Peter Milligan